McCANN, MARKS & ME

Be careful what you wish for

T.A. Bannon

Copyright © T.A. Bannon 2021
This book is sold subject to the condition that it shall not, by way of trade or otherwise, be lent, resold, hired out, or otherwise circulated without the publisher's prior consent in any form of binding or cover other than that in which it is published and without a similar condition including this condition being imposed on the subsequent publisher.
The moral right of T.A. Bannon has been asserted.
ISBN-13: 9798766736219

While all the stories in this book are true, some names and identifying details have been changed to protect the privacy of the people involved.

For Tony,
Who picked up the pieces,
Sadly missed.

CONTENTS

CHAPTER 1 *Bray* *1*
CHAPTER 2 *Paris* *32*
CHAPTER 3 *England* *49*
CHAPTER 4 *Kilcoole* *70*
CHAPTER 5 *Kerry* *103*
CHAPTER 6 *Belfast* *121*
CHAPTER 7 *Kenya* *132*
CHAPTER 8 *Loosdrechtsedijk* *160*
CHAPTER 9 *Ibiza* *171*
CHAPTER 10 *Untersuchungshaftanstalt* *181*
ABOUT THE AUTHOR 218

CHAPTER 1

Bray

Have you ever wondered, in an odd daydreaming moment, what would happen if you wished really hard for something, and then, miraculously, you actually got what you had wished for? Have you also ever wondered what you would wish for if you could only wish for one thing and know with absolute certainty that your one wish would come true? Then, having gotten your one wish, have you ever wondered how that might all turn out? Would it be good or bad? Would you love it or hate it and how would you then deal with the consequences of either of those outcomes? Well, I had wished long, and apparently hard enough, and my one wish had actually come true, or so it had appeared at the outset.

I had lost count of the many idle daydreams I used to have before I met him, trying to decide what my one wish should be. Then suddenly I knew what I actually wanted, or thought I did at any rate. How many times I had thought about what I should do and tried to think what all the possible outcomes could be, well that was hard to say with any accuracy. I had considered all the possibilities that I could think of before making the momentous decision based on all the information

I had at the time. But, as I was to find out later, what I had actually known before making my life-changing decision was miniscule. I was fifteen and a half when this all began, no longer a child but not an adult either, just sort of stuck in that odd space between the two. In the 1960s I'm not really sure they had invented teenagers yet. How long would this phase last and when would I know that I had safely navigated my way to adulthood? Well, who knew the answer to that one? Certainly not me.

I was just about to take my exams at the convent school where I had been studying for the previous five years. My hope was to go to Art college. I had a lot of free time on my hands during this period as I only had to attend the lessons that I was actually taking exams in and could miss all the others and do revision either in school or at home.

You are no doubt wondering, at this point in my narrative, what I had wished for. Well, I had thought about money but that just led to so many questions about what I would spend it on that I had given that idea up. It would be so much easier if I could have the traditional three wishes. Anyway, if I wanted to be an artist, I think at some point I was supposed to be struggling and penniless or maybe that was only if I lived in an attic in Paris.

Then there were all the things that were impossible to quantify, like happiness, who could judge what lifelong happiness would be like, would you get bored with that and just occasionally wish for a few minutes of misery just to break the day up a bit?

Then I had pondered the age-old question: what if I met the perfect man, would we sail of into the sunset together and be blissfully happy for the rest of our lives? According to all the films and books that I had read or watched, it was pretty much all down to the first kiss. If that went well then everything after seemed to be perfect, no problems at all for the rest of our lives. I did wonder though how many frogs you had to kiss before you found the right one. I had also lost count of the many times I had imagined my perfect man; tall, yes definitely, dark hair too, preferably curly, also definitely handsome, absolutely had to be drop-dead gorgeous. I had never decided whether I preferred light or dark eyes, would have to wait and see when he turned up. Slim would be good too, other than that I wasn't too fussy. Then one fine, spring day, he had turned up out of the blue and in the most unlikely of circumstances, having whisked me off my feet, now here we were living the dream. Or were we?

Jim had first appeared in my life two years previously and yes, he was tallish, dark haired, and handsome-ish but not that slim, more stocky, and I had loved him long before our first kiss.

But was mere physical attraction enough to sustain any sort of long-term relationship? We had had one summer together before life had torn us apart.

Now, eighteen long months later, here we were back together, though not how I had ever in my wildest dreams imagined it would be.

After our enforced delay and separation in the course of true love, I had at last ended up living with him in a small Irish town called Bray just down the coast from Dublin. But what should have been the answer to my dreams was rapidly becoming the stuff of nightmares.

In my daydreams I had always imagined just the two of us living in some cosy love nest in some idyllic location, never factoring in the rest of his life. What about his brothers and sisters? What about his parents and the rest of his relatives and friends?

Now here I was on another beautiful summer's day wasting my time daydreaming about how things could be. Along with all the "if onlys" there was now the reality of what life with Jim really was going to be like, at least for the time being.

I wondered what would have been if I hadn't come to Ireland, would Jim have come back to England? Knowing what I knew now, that would almost certainly have been impossible.

I wondered would things be different if Jim and I had a place of our own. We had both changed in the time that we had been forced to be apart and adjusting to now living with his brother and his brother's fiancé was a strange and totally alien experience for me. I sometimes felt embarrassed when we were alone together.

When we had been in England, our relationship had been boyfriend and girlfriend, going on dates, getting to know each other with very limited opportunities for any sort of physical relationship. As he was older than me there had also been a lot of pressure from my parents about our growing relationship. I still had to be home by 10 p.m. each evening, I had school the following day. Even at weekends I had to be home early. None of it had been easy. I knew I still loved him, but did he still love me as much? Was he regretting me coming to live with him and the effort and risk he and his friends had had to make to get me here?

I had already wasted over half the morning pondering these questions and looked set to waste the rest, plus a good deal of the afternoon as well, I just couldn't seem to get motivated when he wasn't around.

Jim was away for a few days and having nothing better to do I was lazing on the couch in front of the large bay window overlooking the seafront at Bray on this beautiful late Spring, early Summer morning. Whenever Jim was away, I slumped into a mild depression, missing him so badly and just counting the hours until he returned. The loneliness I felt without him was not helped by the fact that his brother and the fiancé would ignore me the whole time.

I had turned the couch around to gaze at the view; it having previously been with its back to the window and thus sideways on to the fireplace. I could never understand why people covered up lovely views with ugly furniture and this furniture was certainly ugly. The couch and matching armchairs had clearly been purchased from that exclusive Irish store run by trained, blind leprechauns with no sense of smell whatsoever. They specialised in vomiting on perfectly good fabric, mixing it with manure and then dancing on it until it dried in – they then turned the entire unholy mess into eye-catching furniture.

You could also purchase matching carpets and curtains and the owners of this house had clearly invested in them many years ago. The equally hideous wallpaper added to the general ambience by providing a nauseous smell that attacked your nostrils the moment you entered the house and continued to do battle with your nasal passages until a good half hour after you had left it. Years of stale cooking smells were ingrained in the very fabric of the place and lack of sufficient cleaning had left the whole house in a very sorry state.

The room itself was a good size, also containing an unused dining table and chairs. The rest of the house was furnished in a similar fashion with an accompanying smell. It was a decent sized mid-terraced property that could have been a lovely family home (if anyone had cared for it), but years of neglect, disinterested tenants, and an absent landlord had all left their disfiguring marks on the place.

Bray itself is pleasant enough, an Irish seaside town about twelve miles south of Dublin on the east coast of Ireland, which, over the years, had outgrown its origins as a small fishing village. There is a mile-long beach that starts at the harbour at Bray Head at the northern end and runs south to Greystones with a promenade of shops and restaurants.

The main change to Bray, according to the guidebooks, had been the railway, which had reached Bray in the mid-

1800s, bringing with it the Dublin middle classes for days out to the seaside. With greater use of cars came further expansion, turning Bray and the surrounding area into a dormitory town for Dublin. In the 1950s, tourism from Britain boosted the economy and people who had survived the war came to Ireland on holidays to escape the rationing that continued at home.

The 1960s changed Bray's fortunes yet again as cheap air travel saw tourists departing in their droves for newly accessible foreign climes with guaranteed wall to wall sunshine.

Bray now felt like a ghost town, only busy at weekends when the commuters stopped their commuting for a few days and stayed at home in Bray, taking the time to admire what was around them before racing off to the next exciting thing.

Bray waited, snoozing, to see how the nearly here 1970s would affect its fortunes.

I knew just how Bray felt.

What was I doing here?

Such a small sentence. So many questions contained in so few words. I was here because I had wished for the man of my dreams, and I had gotten him, and here is where he was.

What had I been doing since I got here? Absolutely nothing, and that was becoming a problem.

I had spent the last weeks and months since Jim had been forced to flee England wishing to be with him and fearing that it might never happen.

Now it had at last happened and I was left with the consequences of that wish. Being in Bray was not so bad. True, it was run-down and had seen far better days, but it was the seaside and I had never lived so close to a seaside before.

I could walk to the beach every day and had quickly grown to love watching the waves. It was still a bit too cold to swim but I lived in hope of warm summer weather coming soon.

What I had not anticipated in my worst nightmares when I left my home, my life, and everything I had previously known behind me a few short weeks before, to be with Jim, was that we would end up sharing a house with his relatives, and especially not these particular ones.

The relatives, namely his brother Sean and Sean's no-longer-girlfriend-now-fiancée Oonagh, had hated me from day one. I had no idea why. They had not even tried to get to know me and, if they had tried, I am sure they would still have found some reason imagined or not to hate me.

Jim was the eldest son in a large family and was continually being called upon to sort out all the family's problems and their lives. Maybe Sean thought my presence would alter the relationship he had with Jim, but surely Jim had had girlfriends before. I had given up trying to fathom what the problem might be. I thought back to when I had first met his brother Sean in England when he had come over to visit Jim who was living there at the time. Sean had been welcomed into my home and family and although he was very quiet, the hostility was evident from those first few meetings.

The pleasure of meeting Oonagh had been saved for when I got to Bray.

Now that Jim and I had been unexpectedly re-united and we were all living under the same roof, the hostility from them both was saved mostly for when Jim was out of the house.

When Jim was home, Sean and Oonagh played happy families, but the second the door closed behind him, I became invisible. That suited me just fine and I was happy to ignore the both of them too, but I could not live like this forever.

Jim had left that morning to the sounds of me begging "please don't leave me here with them again, I can't stand it". He had promised to be back as soon as he could but he could never guarantee how long he would be away. I was rapidly becoming a person I did not recognize after only a few weeks. I was used to having a group of friends and going out all the time. I had been studying at Art college and sharing a house with four other girls there was never a dull moment. Now I was doing nothing for days on end and just felt myself becoming more needy by the day. What would I be like after a few more months of this? I had to pull myself together and figure out what I could do to sort this situation out before it turned me into a total head case.

The house we were now all living in had been rented by Jim, as had the business that Sean and Oonagh were running – a fish and chip café on the promenade.

Oonagh was a few years older than me. We were similar height and similar build but where my hair was mid brown and mid length and poker straight, her hair was a luxuriant black with beautiful natural curls tumbling down her back.

I so loved curly hair, a must on my wish list. What if Jim had had straight hair, would I have still fancied him, though he kept his hair short, so it was not so easy to see the curls?

Oonagh and Sean had become engaged in the time that Jim and I had been apart. Fiancée – such an odd word, so many connotations. In this house it was always used by them to distinguish the difference as they saw it between me and Oonagh. My main understanding of that word had been to mean 'the person you were engaged to and intended to marry but who you did not have sex with as you were saving yourself for the big day'.

The Irish-Catholic interpretation varied in their case to mean people who ignored the commandment about saving yourself for marriage but spouted religion generally and especially in my direction as Jim and I were not engaged.

Still, anything apparently could be sorted by a quick trip to the confessional and then back home to start sinning all over again, ready for the next confession. I, on the other hand, apart from the engaged bit, whilst being in exactly the same situation in the same house, was only ever referred to as Jim's girlfriend, as though another girlfriend would come along any minute.

Yes, it did annoy me.

When I first arrived in Bray, I had tried very hard to get along with the two of them, not fully understanding what the problem was.

Several times I went down to the café and tried to help out but they both made it very clear that they did not want me around. I was becoming increasingly lonely, spending entire days and nights on my own while Jim was away.

When he was at home, they complained to him that I was not helping. It was turning into a battleground, and I couldn't see my way out of it.

At first, I thought they were just jealous, they wanted Jim all to themselves. He did everything for them, providing the house and business, and with me around they would lose a certain amount of influence. If that had been the only problem, I could have worked on it, but when I realised that their hatred stemmed from my nationality, I knew there was nothing I could do to change things.

They were Northern Irish Catholics, I was British; nothing any of us could do about that and with all-out conflict breaking out in Belfast again, things were only going to get worse.

I reminded myself once more of the lengths that Jim had gone to in getting me here and the risks some of his friends had taken for me.

With these thoughts foremost in my mind, I roused myself from the couch and decided to go for a walk up to Bray Head to try and clear my head.

Just as I was about to leave the house, the phone rang.

It was Jim. He would be home that evening he said. He could finish his business early.

I was so happy I shrieked down the phone, "Thank you, thank you, I can't wait! I love you, I love you, I love you."

Laughing, he had put the phone down, saying, "If I don't hang up now I'll never get back."

I decided to go on my walk anyway, there would be time to do that and get ready before he got back.

Jim would be home tonight; I was so happy.

I would speak to him then and try and explain how unhappy I was and what was happening in the house while he was away.

I knew he wouldn't be happy about it, but I was completely out of options, something had to change, and quickly. I couldn't continue in this atmosphere any longer.

I walked up the hill to the top of Bray Head. The views from there are spectacular. The entire beach and town were laid out in front of me, with sunlight glittering on the sea. I could almost imagine being happy here.

That illusion was gone before I was halfway back down the hill. The enormity of the conversation I needed to have with Jim weighing heavily on my mind. I hated confrontation and as it involved his family it was going to be even more difficult. I did not want to end up in the middle of a family battle. Nor did I want Jim to think I was asking him to take sides.

I continued my walk along the seafront. I had been walking almost the entire afternoon, putting off the moment I had to return for as long as possible, but now I was getting tired, so reluctantly I turned to head back to the house.

I couldn't think of it in terms of 'going home', only as returning to where Jim was.

Would that 'going home' feeling ever come back while I was here in Bray, or even in Ireland for that matter? I did hope so, and sooner rather than later. I had given up everything to be here, now I wanted to belong here too.

It was early evening before I got back to the house.

Jim had said he would be back about seven o'clock, so I decided to take a quick bath and get changed, not that I had much of a choice about what to wear.

I had left England in secret, with only the clothes I stood up in, the usual student uniform of jeans and a t-shirt. It had been the only way to avoid arousing suspicion or being stopped from leaving. I had still been under police protective custody, but this had been reduced a week or two before I left. It was all 'for my own good', as the police had been fond of telling me. Jim was a dangerous man. Not to me he wasn't.

My first few nights in Ireland were spent with Jim in a Dublin hotel and, after our long-enforced separation, it had been like a honeymoon getting to know each other again; so much had happened in the time we had been apart.

One evening we met some of Jim's friends for a meal at a local restaurant. The food was good, the wine was flowing, and Jim was in his element. A natural raconteur he loved being the centre of attention and that night was no exception.

He was just getting to the good part of his story, one I had heard before, when the manager appeared behind Jim's chair and bent to say something in his ear.

Jim stood up, grabbed my hand, and said, "We have to go now."

Something in his tone and look told me now was not the time to argue or to ask questions so I just stood up and let him lead me away from the table.

We followed the manager through doors marked 'Private, staff only' until we found ourselves in the street somewhere behind the restaurant.

We could hear sirens and the sounds of a commotion at the front of the restaurant.

I was aware that, as we had been leaving, our table in the restaurant was being cleared of our plates, chairs rearranged, and everything made to look as though only six people had been at that table, not eight.

The other diners carried on eating as though nothing out of the ordinary was occurring.

A car was waiting for us a few streets away and we had been whisked away to Bray.

During those couple of days, I had bought a few clothes, but I would need to do some serious shopping sometime soon.

These simple practicalities had not really occurred to me before I left my home, as my departure had been so sudden and unexpected.

I was also running out of money rapidly and that was something else we needed to discuss. I was used to earning my own money and making my own decisions, even though I was only seventeen, but now I was here in Ireland I wouldn't be able to access my bank account.

I had been living away from home while I had been attending Art college and working part time as a barmaid to pay my way.

I lay soaking in the bubbles and must have dozed off with the afternoon's sea air still in my lungs, the fresh aroma just about holding its own before the wallpaper smell could manage to ooze its way in.

Jim had returned.

I hadn't heard him come into the house but was woken instead by him gently kissing my forehead before joining me in the bath. I was saddened by how tired and worn out he looked. He had only been away a few hours but that added to the previous weeks seemed to be really taking a toll on him; my problems could wait for another time. We spent an hour in the bath then went to bed. If any of his family were expecting to see him that night, they were going to be out of luck, I was going to make sure of that.

Sean tried knocking on our bedroom door when they both got back from the café, but Jim just called out that he would speak to him in the morning. Undeterred, Sean tried to carry on a conversation through the closed door, but we were otherwise engaged so just ignored him, eventually he gave up and stomped off in a huff.

We were awake until dawn, only falling asleep as the first rays of morning light were coming in through the window. We slept through Sean and Oonagh getting up for work, with only a vague awareness of them slamming the front door as they left, and we finally got up just after midday.

We had some breakfast and then I suggested a trip into Dublin to stock up on my much-needed new clothes. We had a wonderfully peaceful afternoon of shopping and just being a normal couple for a few short hours. It was good to see the worry leaving Jim's face. Our time together was sometimes very limited, so we had to make the most of it when we could.

We finished our day by having dinner at a restaurant and then headed back to Bray.

As we arrived at the house, Sean and Oonagh were just returning from work. Oonagh eyed my shopping bags. Sean eyed the now happy and relaxed Jim and then they both started with their game of happy families. I eyed them both and thought to myself, *I have managed to keep him away from you two for twenty-four hours without too much difficulty and if I can do it for a day I can do it for a week, or a month. I just have to work out a proper strategy.*

Then I too joined in the game of happy families. I knew they would make me suffer for our day out, but I hoped that when they did, I would see it coming and when they tried to get their revenge I would be prepared.

There had been a lot of catching up to do between Jim

and Sean and, listening to them chat, I began to understand more of what Jim was actually involved in and just how involved he was.

The police had told me some details about him but most of them sounded so outrageous that I hadn't really believed it. Listening to the two of them now though I was beginning to think that maybe some of it might be true. Oonagh was bored with it all and went to bed. She already knew all about Jim, or so she thought.

It annoyed me that I knew so little about his life here in Ireland. Although we had met two years earlier, most of those two years we had been forced to spend apart. I had carried on with my life and gone to college as planned, although the daily police escort had been a bit of a hindrance to making new friends. The police were convinced that Jim would try to contact me at some point.

I knew that he would come for me and that, when he did, I would go with him regardless of the consequences. Jim had gone on the run but was eventually caught, not in England but in Ireland. He spent time in prison but eventually escaped. I didn't find out about any of this until I came to Ireland. Jim was rapidly becoming a local folk hero, they were even singing songs about him.

This person they were describing and writing songs about was not the man I knew and loved.

The bit I did know was the real man, not the showman that emerged whenever there was a crowd to impress, or in the case of his family, the organiser. With me he did not have to pretend or put on an act. I loved him just as he was, warts and all. It is difficult to hide your true nature when you are making love to someone. When you really are in tune with another person there is no hiding and no faking it. I think the other person deep down always knows the truth about your true nature.

Later that night we spent some more time practising the making love bit then fell asleep happy.

We woke late again the next morning and the gruesome twosome had already left for work, and I thought for a fleeting moment that this might end up being easier than I had first thought to change the way things were around here. Now I just had to pick the right moment for our talk.

Our late breakfast was interrupted by the doorbell. Then, when Jim had not moved quickly enough to answer it, a thunderous pounding began and continued until Jim opened the door.

I was startled at first, terrified it might be the police, but Jim had looked unconcerned and had gone to answer it. It was another of Jim's brothers, Patrick, on the doorstep looking a bit the worse-for-wear, it was difficult to work out whether this state was the after-effects of a night on the town, or the beginnings of today's boozing taking their toll.

Jim had told me before about his brother's drinking.

This was my first meeting with Patrick and happily he seemed genuinely pleased to meet me. That could, of course, have just been the Guinness effect. I would have to see how he was towards me when he was sober. From the looks of him, though, I had better not hold my breath while waiting to find out.

Patrick was an attractive man, better looking than Jim in some ways, but the alcohol was already making its mark on his features, and I wondered what he would look like in a few years' time if he carried on at his only too apparent current rate of consumption.

My father had changed jobs after an illness and, by the time I was a teenager, he was working as a licensee and I had earned my pocket money for several years collecting empty glasses, so even as a child I had seen my fair share of people with drink problems.

It was going to be interesting to see the brothers together and to be able to note the similarities and/or differences, to watch the rivalries, if any existed, and to see how they would deal with them.

They all had a strong family likeness. All of the brothers I had seen so far had dark curly hair, although each with differing degrees of curliness. All of them were well-built but apparently the younger brothers, who I had not yet met, were skinny.

I have only one brother and no sisters, so had no experience of what it was like to have competition from the same gene pool with someone of the same sex.

Jim was pleased to see Patrick but was clearly really

unhappy about the state he was in, and I decided to make myself scarce while they talked.

From the bedroom I, and indeed the rest of the street, could hear Jim patiently explaining to Patrick that it was not the best idea in the world to be paralytic at 11 o'clock in the morning and arriving at people's houses expecting to stay for the weekend. I had a quick bath and got dressed, although from the sound of the tirade I could have soaked for a lot longer.

Eventually I went back to the kitchen where the yelling had died down a bit. Jim was running out of steam at last, so I put the kettle on.

By the time it had boiled, relative calm had returned, and we all sat and had coffee, and over the next couple of hours started sobering Patrick up.

By a little after lunch time, he was looking better, although complaining of a headache, not from the booze, but from Jim's brotherly advice being directed at him from a distance of only a few inches away from his eardrum. Jim put Patrick to bed then got dressed, and we headed off to the café as he wanted to see how the business had been doing.

While Jim worked his way through the books, I took a proper look around. It was not a bad little place, a bit dated but with effort it could be a good business. Sean and Oonagh were overjoyed to welcome me into their establishment and were eager to show me everything.

Ok, so they weren't really, but they put on a good show

for Jim's benefit, and it amused me to play along.

This was the first time I had been able to see the whole café. On previous occasions when I had been there, they had both been so hostile that I had left after only a few minutes. I had been unsure of myself and my position in this extended family, and as the newest member I had not wanted to rock the boat.

That had now all changed after my success over them the previous day.

Books looked over and chit-chat finished, Jim and I went for a stroll along the seafront where we stopped at the amusements to play a few games. Jim was very competitive and being the eldest was used to winning, as was I. Neither of us would give in at whatever we were doing without a good battle. We had a go on a few of the machines then headed to the rifle range.

I put up a good show and mortified Jim by beating him on the rifle range. He didn't know that I had spent a lot of time in the previous weeks practising. I had to tell him that in the end otherwise we would have been there all night while he tried beat me. I for my part was happy to stay as long as possible but knew that I was only postponing the inevitable, so I let him win a game. Eventually, honour restored, we headed back to the house.

By the time we got back, Patrick was awake and had washed and changed. He looked even more handsome. The three of us were going to go out to dinner that night so, while

Jim changed, I had my first proper chat with the now reasonably sober Patrick. I discovered I had made my first friend. He realised that I had interceded on his behalf with Jim and thanked me for calming Jim down. I, for my part, made it clear to Patrick that I agreed with what Jim had said to him, I was just not in the habit of getting a message across to someone directly in front of me in a volume that would also get the message across to the rest of the street.

We had a very pleasant meal in a local restaurant and then went to the pub. I wasn't sure if the pub was such a good idea, but Patrick seemed to be trying hard to behave. We all had a fantastic night. Patrick was as charismatic as Jim and the two of them kept the whole pub going with stories and jokes the whole time, interspersed with songs and the occasional dance to give them a chance to get their voices back. Yelling at Patrick earlier had left Jim a little hoarse and he had nearly lost his voice altogether by the time we headed back to the house. The end of another good day.

Tomorrow was Sunday and for me it was the worst day of the week. The café was closed as were all the other shops so the other two would be at home all day. Nothing much happened on a Sunday, you could go to church all morning if you wanted to. This was followed by lunch, then more church in the afternoon and so on, into the evening. The prayers were always said so fast that all the words blended into one continuous drone that could be anything and mean anything, but inevitably ended up meaning nothing at all. The words ceased to be heard individually, they just blurred into what sounded like the hum of so many thousand bees going up and down in a strange unison.

Then, when it suddenly stops, everyone shakes themselves from the stupor that has engulfed them and as though waking from a trance, they stand up and leave. The droning sound being replaced by the clattering of rosary beads being put away, ready for next time. I was amazed they didn't all have calluses on their knees the amount of time they spent kneeling on them. I had attended mass once since I had been here but had found no comfort in the familiar ritual. Thanks to my family upbringing, I knew what it meant to be a Catholic in England, it was just magnified in Ireland; still, if you have been on the booze all Saturday night, Church on a Sunday was as good a place as any for a snooze, it being hard to hear a snore above the drone of so many prayers being said.

I was the first awake on that Sunday morning, so I set too and cleared the kitchen, tidied the sitting room, and by the time I had finished everyone else was awake, so I started making breakfast. Sean and Oonagh joined the three of us and appeared to be making an effort; perhaps Patrick had said something to them.

Jim and I were going to go for a drive down the coast in the afternoon. The others did not want to come but Oonagh was going to do a roast dinner for all of us, so we agreed to be back in time.

Oonagh was, in fact, a really good cook so we were looking forward to our meal.

I had not yet mastered the art of getting all the ingredients for a meal ready and on the table at the same time. My cooked breakfast was OK, but a decent roast dinner is altogether a different story. I admired her skill and if things had been different, we could have been good friends.

After breakfast Jim and I drove for a while down the coast away from Bray, past Greystones, the next small village, and onwards. It was a beautiful day again and I was loathe to spoil the atmosphere by telling Jim how unhappy I truly was here.

Jim turned the car into a narrow lane that eventually led to a shingle beach. The water glistened in front of us and ran for miles in either direction. Grey waves were breaking over the shingle as we left the car and started walking along the breakwater.

Was this still the English Channel or were we far enough down the coast to be looking at the ocean, I wondered. I was silent, pondering what I should do, when Jim interrupted my thoughts by asking me if I had noticed the house halfway down the lane on the left-hand side, and if I had, what did I think of it.

I had seen it and thought how lovely it looked. It was a double-fronted cottage with a large garden in front. When I told him this, he was really pleased and said he had just rented it for us as our first real home together.

I couldn't believe it, I just started to cry; all the stress of the last few weeks caught up with me. Jim made no attempt to stop me, he just stood there, cuddling me until I stopped crying of my own accord. He knew I had been unhappy but had just thought I was homesick.

I explained what had been happening with Oonagh and Sean while he was away, but before we left the beach, I made him promise that he wouldn't argue with them over it. I did not want a family argument to start that would drag on forever. We would have our own first home soon and I just wanted to be happy.

We returned to Bray in plenty of time for our roast dinner. Oonagh had made lamb with all the trimmings and a fantastic gravy; it was really delicious, and I had no hesitation in telling her so.

She looked at me dubiously and then seemed to decide that I was telling the truth, I really had enjoyed dinner and we all appreciated the effort that had gone into cooking it.

Jim was quiet but with Patrick around to keep the talk going it wasn't as noticeable as it might have been, Jim didn't mention anything about the new house, so neither did I. As nobody asked what Jim and I had been doing all afternoon it was easy to avoid the subject. I always hated to have to lie and as Jim had not told them about our day, I assumed he didn't want them to know yet. When he did eventually speak, he said he had to go back to Belfast on Monday morning but would be back on Tuesday evening. As soon as he told me this, it spoiled the rest of Sunday evening, I said I had a headache and went to bed early. He followed me to the bedroom and said, "I've asked Patrick to stay on an extra couple of days to keep you company."

"What?" I couldn't believe it. "What if he is as bad as the other two? As soon as your back is turned then I'll have three of them on my case." He promised me that Patrick would not be like them.

"He likes you," Jim assured me.

"Well, we will just have to wait and see."

Jim left in the middle of Monday morning after Sean and Oonagh had gone to work so it wasn't possible to tell if there had been any change in attitude with them or if it had still been an act for Jim's benefit. I would have to wait until they got back this evening to find out. I wasn't holding my breath though.

I made sandwiches for myself and Patrick at lunchtime, he had gotten up late morning and now sober was as pleasant and friendly as he had been when drunk. Things were getting better all round and would be even better as soon as we moved. I hoped that would be as soon as possible.

While we were eating, an odd noise kept interrupting our conversation, we could hear strange scratching noises in the kitchen. Something was moving about so I grabbed a mop, Patrick grabbed a saucepan, and we started a search, eventually narrowing the source of the noise down to the cooker.

Patrick took up position standing behind the cooker door with me brandishing the mop in front. He quickly yanked open the oven door, while I stood ready to attack whatever was inside with the mop. For such a big guy he had managed to stay out of the danger zone of whatever was inside by offering to open the door and was now safely hiding behind it while I was left standing in front waiting to be attacked by whatever was lurking inside with only a mop for protection. Nothing jumped out, thankfully. I saw the roasting tin with the leftover lamb still in it, now contained in a pool of congealed fat, and sitting in the middle of the fat along with the lamb was a little brown mouse, munching on the leftover meat. It looked so cute twitching its whiskers and watching me and waiting to see what I was going to do. Cleary it was not a mouse that was afraid of a mop.

Then I suddenly realised yes, I was meant to be doing something.

I made a grab for the mouse, but I wasn't quick enough to catch it, and it scampered through a small hole at the back of the oven and disappeared.

The leftover lamb and bone had obviously been left in the tin overnight instead of being put in the fridge. There were droppings in the fat with small footprints making a number of little trails. Either one mouse had made lots of visits or there was a whole army of them gorging on this feast. I took the roasting tin out of the oven and left the tin with its grizzly contents on the work surface by the sink along with what I hoped was a polite note for Oonagh ready for when she returned from work, explaining about the mice.

Patrick and I then went out for the afternoon.

Patrick and I were getting on so well and having such a laugh that we stayed out late into the evening. We had started the afternoon with a trip to the amusements then had walked along the promenade window shopping and chatting. It was really good to have a friend to do things with, I had been missing the simple things of life. We had dinner at a small restaurant and then went to the pub.

Patrick did drink but not to excess and I really enjoyed our day and evening out. By the time we got back to the house, Sean and Oonagh had already gone to bed. On the Tuesday morning I had gotten up early to go into Dublin, I was excited about the house Jim had rented but he had said it only had a few bits of furniture so I was going to buy some things for our first home together, although how I would explain to the others what all the new stuff was for, I hadn't quite worked out yet.

So once again I missed the gruesome twosome. The bus took forever to get to Dublin. I made a mental note to check how long the train took, it had been so much quicker by car, maybe I should think about learning to drive.

I spent a happy day looking around the shops picking up a few interesting bits and pieces for our new home. I found a few prints, some cushions, and some bedding. The house had some furniture, so Jim had said we didn't need much but I wanted just a few things to call our own. I had no idea what his taste in home furnishings was, so I didn't go mad with buying too much until I had a chance to discuss it with him properly and until I saw how the house was furnished.

I headed back to the bus stop in plenty of time to get the early bus to be back before Jim got back from Belfast. Standing at the bus stop and contemplating my afternoon shopping and the prospect of our forthcoming move, a wave of happiness washed over me. Then, just as quickly, a wave of horror when I realized that I had bought single bed sheets instead of double. I dashed back to the shop and made it just before they closed.

My face was red with embarrassment while I tried to explain my mistake to the amused shop assistant. The shopping had taken longer than I expected, not only because I had to go and change the sheets but then I got lost trying to navigate my way back to the bus stop around this new city.

I had then missed the bus back and had to wait for the next one and by the time I did get back Jim's car was already outside the house. As I opened the door of the house, a new and different smell greeted me, although somehow familiar as it smelled a bit like lamb. Strange to have lamb on Tuesday when we had had roast on Sunday, then a horrible thought struck me, maybe Oonagh hadn't seen the note I left her and didn't know about the mice.

I made my way to the kitchen. Oonagh was indeed re-heating Sunday's leftover lamb for tonight's dinner.

I rushed into the kitchen, saying, "I'm so sorry, I left you a note about the lamb."

"Yes, I know," she replied, "I cut off the bits that had been chewed." This was the final straw – I was leaving. I didn't care where I went, I just had to get out of this place. I couldn't stand it a minute longer.

Jim had been sitting at the kitchen table reading the paper, waiting for me and his dinner when I entered the house, and was surprised by the look on my face and the heated argument that now broke out. Weeks of pent-up anger and frustration boiled to the surface, and I realized I was shouting at Oonagh and when Jim tried to intervene, he got an earful as well.

Jim stood between us, completely perplexed, trying to figure out what on earth was going on. "I didn't leave my home and college, my job and my friends and family to come and live in this Hell hole in squalor," I screamed, my anger now directed at him.

He still had a look of surprise on his face which, if I hadn't been so angry, I would have found funny. I don't think he had ever heard me raise my voice to anyone before. He suddenly grabbed both of my arms, pinning them to my sides and hugged me as hard as he could. I could hardly breathe. "I know," he said, "I'm sorry." As he held me the anger gave way, and I began to cry. He let me cry for a few minutes then gently said, "What's made you so angry?"

Where did he want me to begin? I decided to stay in the moment, and I told him about the mouse. He turned to Oonagh and said, "Is this right, did you see the note?" The look on her face was the only answer he needed. Jim said, "Get your things together, we're leaving right now." I went to our bedroom and started to pack. It wasn't going to take long, neither of us had much luggage.

"But where are we going?" I asked Jim when he followed me into the bedroom.

"It doesn't matter," he said, "we can go wherever we want now."

"What do you mean?"

He had picked up my new false passport today and had planned a short holiday for us. He had been keeping it as a surprise in case the passport wasn't ready when he expected it to be, but everything had gone ok, we were leaving that evening.

That was all I needed to hear. I was so relieved that he had already planned on going away, I did not want to be the cause of us leaving Bray, it would have been one more nail in my coffin.

We walked out of that house with the sounds of Oonagh still protesting loudly that the lamb was fine to eat, that she had cut off the bits that the mice had been munching on and thrown away the congealed fat as though that somehow made it OK. Sean said nothing, just stood watching us walking away.

How could these two be running a café?

CHAPTER 2

Paris

Have passport, will travel.

I had never had a passport before as I had never travelled out of England. Apart from the ferry over to Ireland a few short weeks ago to be with Jim, most of the other journeys I had been on had been fairly short: trips to see relatives, random days out to see stately homes, zoo days, or trips to the seaside during school holidays.

We did not really have holidays when I was a child. My family were poor, as were most of our neighbours on the council estate where I grew up, so holidays where you actually travelled to another place and stayed there in hotels or guest houses were unknown to most of us. The only reason we managed to have days out was because in those days my father had a job as a salesman and with that particular job came a van that Dad was allowed to take home and use at the weekends.

Now, as we drove towards the airport, I was so excited and a bit apprehensive. So much was happening so quickly, I'd never imagined what it would be like to go on a plane, pretty soon I was going to find out though. We were definitely going to fly somewhere Jim had said but he was still keeping the destination a secret. I hoped it would be somewhere good and I began to think about where I would choose to go if I had the choice. Thinking about different possible destinations helped to take my mind off the actual flying bit. I didn't know if I was going to be scared or not, what if I hated flying, there would be no getting off once the door was closed. I had wondered why we didn't go to the new house that we had looked at on our Sunday drive which Jim had rented for us but Jim said that it wouldn't be ready for a few weeks, so we were going on a short holiday until it was ready. He had been planning our holiday for a while he said but had just been waiting for my passport to arrive. I looked at my new passport, my new fake passport, and in my mind practised saying my new name. Would I one day have a passport in my real name? Who knew?

I was glad that this day was almost over. I had so hated being in the middle of rows all the time in Bray, I hadn't recognized the person that I had become whilst I had been living there. I thought back to the person who had been screaming at Oonagh, that was not the person I wanted to be or had been in the past. Where had the real me gone? I told Jim again how sorry I was about earlier, he just brushed it off and said, "Don't worry about it. It was never going to work, you're British and Sean and Oonagh would never forgive you for that." I knew all about that now, but they might at least have given me a chance.

The last few rays of sunshine were falling behind the hills ahead of us now. We were driving through the night covered by darkness, which eased my fears a little but not quite enough. Would the new fake passport pass a thorough check? If not, we could both be arrested and then what might happen? I began to worry about flying again. What if we get in the air and I'm terrified? At least I had Jim with me on this first flight as he had been with me for so many other important firsts in my life so far.

For the moment I felt safe in this little metal cocoon racing through the night with Jim at my side and the gruesome twosome left far behind in Bray, and that was enough. I was genuinely sorry that things had ended so badly and although I did not like them, they were his family and he cared about all of them and felt responsible for them. I was sorry to have been the cause of the rift.

I was so completely lost in my own world of worries that I had not been paying attention to anything that Jim had been saying for the last mile or so, but as the lights of the airport up ahead came into view, one word finally filtered through my befuddled, worried brain – PARIS. It stopped my thoughts dead in their tracks. I thought that maybe I had just imagined it, but no, he just said it again – Paris. He was excited about taking me on my first trip to Paris that he hadn't been able to keep it a secret any longer and had just blurted it out. The car nearly left the road as I flung my arms around his neck and started hugging and kissing him. Just the name of the place was enough to excite me – Paris, Paris,

Paris, I was singing over and over again – and now we were actually heading there together. I couldn't quite believe it.

We managed to make it into the car park before I strangled him. He needed both hands to loosen my grip from around his neck I was hugging and kissing him so much. He was happy and laughing to see me so excited but said, "Calm down, calm down. We're at the airport, you need to stay focused." He was right, I needed to focus and remember my new name and date of birth and he needed to remember it too so as not to call me by the wrong name.

"Theresa," I said, then tried it again, "Theresa. Do I look like a Theresa?" I didn't know, what do Theresas normally look like, what did the real Theresa, whose passport I now had, look like? We walked into the airport as casually as possible under the circumstances, I was still so excited about the thought of going to Paris.

While we waited for the flight I sat and thought about my new name. If I had the choice of all the names in the world, would I have chosen Theresa? It had never really occurred to me that I would need to change my name, but the police were looking for Jim and now that I was living with him, they would be looking for me too. Even now I didn't fully realize exactly what Jim was involved in or how involved he was, he had told me about some of it but obviously not all as much for my own safety as his. I couldn't tell anyone else what I didn't know.

Doing my best to stay focussed, we eventually made it through all the checkpoints and suddenly we were safely on board the plane and preparing for take-off. I gripped Jim's hand as the plane began to move. It was exhilarating to feel the speed building up as we headed along the runway and then to realise that, all too quickly, we were in the air. I was glad it was still dark; I wasn't sure that I would have wanted to take my first flight in daylight. I was terrified of heights but at least in the dark I couldn't see how far away the ground was.

Just as I was getting used to the different engine noises and strange vibrations of the plane, it was nearly all over and we were slowly descending towards Paris. With some hesitation, I ventured a look out of the window. It was truly magical. Paris was set out below us, all the streets and houses lit up, the twinkling lights of the city looked like little crystals on a giant chandelier glittering and sparkling in the blackness – maybe they had lit them especially for us.

We took a taxi from the airport into the centre of Paris. Jim had booked us into the George V. This must be good; I had actually heard of this hotel but never imagined that I would actually ever see it, let alone stay in it. The taxi pulled up outside and we disembarked, the taxi door having been opened by a uniformed doorman.

All I could think was *Wake me up, I'm in a dream!* From the stunning art deco façade to the beautiful floral displays in the reception area, the whole building screamed luxury and I loved every inch of it. The whole effect was breath-taking. The scent from the mass of flowers decorating the reception area was intoxicating, although it might not have been so good for my hay fever. I felt as if I were floating through the opulent foyer and upstairs to a room so magnificent I had never seen anything like it before. Even the stately homes we had visited on our family days out at home had never to my mind looked as good as this. The decor was lavish, gold everywhere with hand-painted wallpapers and yards of fabrics and braids decorating every surface. The oil paintings and 17th-century tapestries along with the antique furniture finished the whole vision perfectly – what a contrast from the vision we had just left behind in Bray.

Before I travelled to Ireland, I had been at college training to be a designer, so I could really appreciate how much time and skill had gone into creating the things that now surrounded us. The designs we had been working on at college, however, had been bog standard, the current vogue was for modern bright geometric designs. To now see these traditional beautiful floral masterpieces was a joy. I could have spent the whole night looking at the wallpaper designs, let alone the curtains and furniture. Jim, however, had other ideas. We had a blissful first night in this beautiful place and eventually fell asleep in each other's arms, happy at last. It was everything I had hoped it would be and had been waiting so long for.

When I woke it was really early in the morning, only just light, Jim was still sleeping peacefully beside me. I bounded over to the window to take my first look at daytime Paris. The beautiful curtains caught my eye again and I wrapped myself in them, snuggling into their softness, while I gazed out of the window. They were so thick and plush it was like wearing a beautiful blanket. Paris was before me, the street below slowly waking up. It was a sight I had never imagined that I would ever see in real life.

Ireland had seemed a little different when I had first arrived but still familiar, Paris though was like landing on another planet, everything was strange and new. The shops and café's that I could see from the window looked so different from anything at home. Even at this early hour people were sitting on little tables outside eating breakfast. I couldn't wait to go and explore. I gazed at the Eiffel tower in the distance, lovely to look at from here, I didn't want to climb to the top though, I hoped Jim had already done that. He was an absolute menace for teasing people if he found out they were scared of anything, and he had already found out from the flight that I was scared of heights. I could hear Jim stirring, I hoped he hadn't fully woken yet; I was still wrapped in the curtains and wouldn't be able to make it back to the bed or my clothes without him seeing me. Too late, he was already up on one elbow and looking across at me.

Crazy, I know we had just spent the night together, but I still felt embarrassed to walk about naked in front of him; maybe if I waited a while, he would come over to me.

I stood there trying to look casual, pretending that I was just about to admire the view. He was fully awake now and watching me with a smile on his face; all the while he was making overtures to me, beckoning me to come back to him, there was no doubting his intentions.

It had been so long that we had been apart, and I was so unused to this that Jim just looked funny to me, so I started laughing to cover my embarrassment. He threw the bed pillows at me. Thankfully I grabbed a few and used them to cover myself up before heading to the bed and my clothes. Jim by now was pretending to sulk because I had laughed at him, so he tried to get the pillows away from me. I was not willing to give up my cover without a decent struggle. We had a massive pillow fight, neither one of use willing to give in without a good battle. When we had exhausted ourselves battling over the pillows, we fell onto the bed laughing and I settled into his arms and let him wrap me in the love that I had been missing for so long.

Afterwards we settled down again and talked about all the things we had missed in our enforced time apart and the disappointment I had felt during the time spent in Bray.

It was so good to be able to finally talk to him properly without the feeling that we were being watched and judged all the time.

Bray had been so difficult for so many reasons, not least of all the lack of privacy and the fact that when Jim was at the house everyone wanted a piece of him. I had felt like just another person in the queue, and that had to stop. I realized now that he had responsibilities that would sometimes have to come first, but I still didn't really understand those responsibilities. I was only a child really when I first met Jim and he was very much the adult. I had grown up a lot since those early days, in more ways than one, and I would try to not be embarrassed around him in the future.

From now on we would discuss everything, no matter what. I knew there were some things that he couldn't tell me about, like what he was doing in Belfast. But this was for my own safety, and I understood that now as much as anything and I preferred not to know anyway. Maybe some time in the future, when I felt more secure, we would be able to talk about it, but for the time being I was content just getting to know him again. If we really wanted this to work out, then we couldn't let stupid things like problems with his family come between us. Now we would be equals in our relationship and at last it felt as though we were more of a real couple, not just a mis-matched girlfriend and boyfriend.

Now it was time to see Paris.

We spent the next couple of days exploring Paris and the nights exploring each other. During the day we strolled the narrow streets of Montmartre and one day found ourselves at the church of Sacre Coeur, it seemed it was impossible to get away from religion no matter where you went. The Church was a beautiful building though and I was glad that we had the time to take a look inside. Neither of us attended church anymore, I had stopped going when I had started college and had then had a choice about what I did with my Sunday morning, Jim never wanted to talk about why he stopped. It was only while I had been in Bray that I had gone once or twice as it had seemed to be expected but I had avoided it whenever I could. While I had been living at home there had never been a choice, my parents were both religious as were both of their families and it had been easier to just go and avoid the arguments.

At night we walked around the little bars and cafes that were everywhere, we could eat and drink whenever we wanted, they seemed to be always open, so very different from at home. The sights and smells of these little streets were wonderful to me; the aromas of olive oil, garlic, and strange spices I didn't recognize seemed to rise up from the very pavements themselves. I loved it.

During these days, I began to realise what an odd couple we were. Jim was always well dressed. Handmade suits, beautiful shoes, his wavy black hair well cut, not stylish but business-like, and it suited him, he had that manner about him. I on the other hand looked positively scruffy next to him. My hair was halfway down my back, usually tied back with an elastic band, I would cut odd chunks off now and again whenever it annoyed me or got in my face while I was trying to do something. My clothes were cheap. I was always covered in dye at college so there had been no point in buying expensive things and I couldn't have afforded to buy them anyway. My 'going out' clothes had all been hand-made by me or my friends from the fashion department at the college. After all, we were going to student nights out, so nobody cared much about how their clothes looked.

Walking in the streets around the hotel, looking in shop windows, I marvelled at how much my life had changed in such a short time. I had been used to shopping in cheap fashion shops, rails of clothes stuffed together, piles of things stacked in the windows with sale stickers on them, cheaper still if they were missing buttons. Being able to sew I had gotten a few bargains. Here single items were artistically displayed with no price tags. If you had to ask the price, you couldn't afford it. The doors were kept closed and you had to press a bell to get in. Of course, this only happened after they had inspected you from inside the shop and decided whether they wanted you in their shop or not, then, if you passed muster, they would release the door lock. I did not want to risk pressing the bell – I already knew what their response would be to me. I decided there and then that I needed a new look but what and how would I go about achieving the transformation? This would need some serious consideration. I asked Jim what he thought.

"You always look beautiful to me," he said.

"But I look a mess," I complained.

He decided against arguing, saying instead, "It's up to you, just don't cut your hair too short, I like it long." And then he said, "If you are going shopping, we will be going to a nightclub tomorrow night, you could buy something new to wear for that."

The following day Jim had a few things to do, people to see, etc. So, I had a day to myself, and I decided I would use the time to get a decent haircut and buy some new clothes. There was a beauty salon at the hotel, so I went there. They worked on me for about an hour and a half while I watched my hair disappear and eventually ended up with a shoulder-length style with a soft fringe which made me look older, I thought. I wondered if Jim would like it. They also manicured my fingernails, at least they were no longer stained with dye. I got the impression that the two stylists thought I should have spent the rest of the day at the salon. They obviously seemed to think there was a great deal more that needed doing, but by then I had had enough. I glanced in the mirror at the new me and I wondered what Jim had ever seen in me in the first place if, as these two ladies thought, I needed so much more work doing. Oh well, now for the clothes.

I found several clothing stores underneath a large hotel, the Concorde La Fayette, the ladies at the beauty salon had suggested I might find something suitable here. Obviously, the clothes at the George V would not have been suitable as the ladies at the hair salon had been quick to point out. I was glad that they had, I had taken a quick look before I left and knew what they meant, I would never have felt comfortable wearing what they had on offer. These shops were much more me, I should be able to get everything I needed here. This hotel was a circular tower. more than thirty floors high at a rough guess, very tall compared to other buildings in Paris, with a massive hotel lobby. I had walked into it by mistake while looking for the floor with the shops on. At first, I thought I was in the metro station, then I quickly realised I would have to brush up on my school French if I wanted to find my way around more easily. I bought a few skirts and tops and a dress and shoes for going out that night. The dress was black, strappy, and showed a lot more cleavage than I was used to flashing, but with the new haircut I felt really grown up and yes, maybe even a bit sexy. The shoes were also strappy with heels. I would have to practise walking in them back in the hotel room before we went out; my usual footwear had mainly been trainers. Jim had said that tonight we were going to a burlesque show, whatever that might be, called Crazy Horse.

Back at the hotel I tried out my new outfits then showered and changed into my new dress, I practised walking in my new shoes. The heels were not that high, only a couple of inches, but they still felt really odd after flat shoes. After a short while they started to feel OK and if I went slowly enough I could do it. Walking on carpet was not too bad but now I needed to practise in the bathroom to see what it felt like on a slippery floor. I would have to make it across the expanse of the marble floor in the hotel reception without landing on my behind.

I heard Jim return, calling my name to check if I was back as he entered the room. "Just a minute," I called from the bathroom. Then I slowly exited the bathroom, trying to look as elegant as I possibly could. He stopped abruptly in the middle of the bedroom, and I thought for a second that he was going to turn around and leave. He had this surprised look on his face, as though he had walked into the wrong room by mistake. He slowly realised he was not mistaken and just stood looking at me. I could not figure out whether he liked the new look or not, I had never seen Jim speechless before. I stopped walking and we just stood looking at each other. As the moments ticked by, he looked into my eyes, and

I looked into his. Neither of us said a word, but it felt as though a lifetime of conversations passed between us in those moments, all the things we had missed in the time we had been apart. Then slowly we moved towards each other and gently embraced, both of us too emotional to speak. I had been so young when we first met, just a girl, so many things had happened in between, now he was looking at a woman.

We left the George V to meet Jim's business friends at the Crazy Horse. He walked slowly and I held his arm to steady myself as we negotiated the slippery reception area, I had made him promise that if I had to walk anywhere, he would make sure that he was close enough for me to take his arm. The doorman got us a taxi. It was not far to the club, but I didn't feel confident enough to manage a walk along the uneven pavements. In the taxi Jim surprised me by saying that the Crazy Horse was a strip club. My head reeled. *What! I am only seventeen and not even legally old enough to drink!* Did I really want to go to some sleazy club and watch women take their clothes off? Jim laughed and said, "It's not like that, wait and see. Anyway, your passport says you are older than you are." I couldn't argue with that.

The club was packed with every table taken, but luckily Jim's friends had booked, so we headed for our table near to the stage. It was right at the front of the room, centre of the stage, dam I had been hoping to be able to hide somewhere near the back of the room in the shadows. Jim introduced me to his friends, another two couples, they seemed pleasant enough, maybe it wouldn't be so bad after all. The woman I sat next to had been here a few times before and she assured me that it was a really good show, and the food was good too. I was surprised at how civilised it seemed, with couples at the other tables having dinner before the show. Not what I had expected at all. We had a good steak and at about 11 p.m. the show began. The curtains went up to reveal a chorus line of female dancers doing a version of the cancan. They looked incredible as they were all exactly the same height. The chorus line came on in different costumes between each act, their costumes slowly becoming skimpier as the show went on. After about their third appearance, I realised the reason they were of identical heights was because the heels on their shoes were all different thicknesses and the costumes had been adjusted so that they made one continuous line when they all stood together. It looked amazing.

The first featured artiste came on stage, and I thought to myself that this was going to be a quick act as she did not have much on to start with. I was not at all sure how I felt about this whole event. While I was attending college, there had been the beginnings of the women's lib movement starting up which had quickly escalated into a massive movement demanding change in all walks of life and occupations, this, plus the pro-abortion lot holding rallies on a regular basis, had heralded a huge change in peoples thinking about the role of women in society. As I had been brought up as a Catholic, the pro-abortion bit was something I really needed to get my head around, years of indoctrination were hard to overcome and trying to take an objective look at both sides of the argument had proved to be really difficult. I was still unsure how I actually felt about it. Likewise, women's liberation. I had been attending an Art college which was probably 90% male but there had been no barrier to me attending, maybe life was different in other jobs. I did, however, have fairly strong views about women and girls being objectified although I didn't think that burning bras was the way forward. Change needed to happen and the sooner the better, I just wasn't sure what was the best way to go about it. And having said all that here I was sitting in a club about to watch a woman remove her clothes, well after this at least I would know what I was talking about having actually seen a strip show.

The performance continued on stage with a large rope being suspended from one side of the stage to the other. The female performer artfully removed her clothes whilst balancing on the rope. At first, I felt a bit embarrassed, but as she continued, I began to realise just how graceful and athletic her performance was. So practised that she could have been an Olympic gymnast, balancing on her rope, her movements synchronised to the music, it was just that she was taking her clothes off at the same time – now that was some skill. The following acts were equally good and just as skilful but the woman on the rope was the one that impressed me the most. I had weird visions of the washing line at home springing into my mind, must have been the alcohol but no, I was pretty sure it wouldn't take my weight. I would have to make sure we had a good strong one at the new house so that I could get some practise in although I was also pretty sure it would be beyond me. We had had the most wonderful night and we made it back to the hotel just in time for breakfast.

Jim and I would have many more trips to Paris over the next few years but this was the only one where we would stay at the George V, and it had been magical, everything that I had ever dreamed Paris would be.

On future trips we regularly stayed at the Concorde La Fayette. It was very modern compared to the George V but was more business-like, so it was better for when Jim had to meet people and you could then blend with the crowds on the shopping levels and quickly exit from various access points around the building should the need arise.

This first trip was over too quickly and now we were heading back to Ireland, but we were going back to our first home as a couple, and we were a much stronger couple than we had been when we left. I liked the new me, not only my hair and clothes but the confidence that had come with the outward embellishments. Not only did I like the new me, Jim did as well, telling me, "You are with me now, don't let my family or anyone else get you down. We don't have to explain our relationship to anyone else, it is none of their business." I certainly hoped that would be the case, although experience of the others had left me thinking that it would not all be the plain sailing that Jim was imagining. I hadn't met his mother yet and thought that her reaction to me would probably be closer to what Sean's reaction had been than to what Patrick's had. Oh well, time would tell.

CHAPTER 3

England

Our flight was in daylight this time and I decided to sit near the window and for the first time look at France from the air. The initial fear about how high up we were, was quickly overtaken by the fascination with all the things that I could see from here. Looking at clouds and then flying through them to a mysterious world beyond where we seemed to be floating in nothingness was an extraordinary feeling. I tried to take in every sensation and hold it in my thoughts, hoping to one day be able to talk to friends who had never flown and be able to describe it to them.

As our plane crossed over England on the way back to Ireland, my thoughts were drawn back to my home and what I had left behind a few months ago. It felt as though a lifetime had passed in those few short months. I had grown up a lot in such a short space of time. As I watched the chequerboard of small fields pass below us, I thought about my family and how they were coping with my sudden disappearance. When Jim had gone on the run, my parents had given the standard parental advice, 'you need to forget about him now, concentrate on your studies.' No-one really listened when I told them I knew he would come back for me apart from the police that is, they had put me under an armed guard from day one. When I had finally managed to escape, I had left a note for my parents telling them that I was going of my own free will and would keep in touch with them when I could. I had no idea where or how Jim was living; he had only managed to get a few brief messages to me in the time we had been apart. I had tried to make regular contact with my parents since I left to reassure them that I was ok. But it had been difficult to make regular phone calls and I was always aware that their phone was being tapped so the calls could only be really short to try and avoid the police being able to trace where the call was coming from. They seemed to be coping alright although I did worry about my father and how my sudden departure might have affected his health.

When I was very young, my father had TB and had to have a lung removed. He had recovered but would always carry the legacy of such a serious illness. It was this illness though that had changed the course of my early life. Our family moved from the post-war slums of the northern industrial city of my birth to a less urban environment so that he could recover. Just before a really hard winter we relocated to an isolated farmhouse on the outskirts of a small southern city. Life was really tough for us all in the first few weeks that we lived there. The farmhouse was set back from the road in the middle of a field and a few days after we arrived, we were snowed in. We had all been used to the hustle and bustle of a large city surrounded by a large extended family; here we were surrounded by fields, you could go for days without seeing anyone. My mother in particular hated it. The isolation was bad enough, being cooped up all day with two young children in a house infested with mice nearly finished her. We eventually moved into a shared house on the fringes of the city. We had the ground floor; another family had the first floor. My mother took in lodgers to make ends meet. My father had recovered reasonably well by then and was able to work again.

Following slum clearances after the Second World War, large housing estates were being built around the edges of the city and we were allocated a three-bedroom maisonette; for the first time in my life, I would have a bedroom of my own. We moved in with high expectations for our new lives and considered ourselves fortunate to have a lovely new home. Sadly, these expectations for a better existence were not to be realised. In the early days the houses were well-maintained; we even had an on-site caretaker but the money that had been available post-war to build the homes was not available to maintain them as we went into the 1960s. The estate became known as a sink estate. The original tenants dwindled, those who could get out did. We were stuck there. Most of the new people being housed there had all been evicted from somewhere else and were resentful of having to live on the estate, they also brought with them all the problems that had led to their evictions from their previous homes.

Nothing much was expected of anybody who lived on the estate. Leave school for those who bothered to go in the first place, get a lousy job again for those who bothered or live a life on benefits for those who didn't and hope to get housed on a better estate one day. Life on the estate was to be endured, not enjoyed.

The next major change in my life occurred when I was eleven: my eleven plus exam. A pass meant going to a grammar school, then taking O level examinations with the possibility to go on to college or university. A fail meant going to the local comprehensive, taking O level examinations at sixteen, then mainly a manual job or maybe something secretarial.

When I took my eleven plus exam, nothing much was expected of me; I wasn't considered particularly bright. My younger brother was the brainbox, so it came as a considerable surprise to everyone, including me, when I passed. This meant that I would now be going to the local convent grammar school on a scholarship. The school fees would be paid by the scholarship, but my parents would have to find the money for the rigid inflexible Winter and Summer school uniforms plus all of the sports kits etc. It was going to be a costly enterprise to send me to the grammar school.

Overnight I became neither fish nor fowl, ostracised by my contemporaries on the estate who had not passed the exam, especially when I started at the convent and had to walk to school wearing white gloves and a boater with a long yellow cotton dress in the Summer, or a felt hat gloves and blazer in the Winter, there was no hiding the uniform or what it signified. Then when I went to school I was mostly ignored by the other pupils who had all been to prep school together and were suspicious of anyone who might be attending their school due to brains rather than money.

My eventual saving grace was being good at sport; if they wanted to win, it was good having me on the team. Academically I still didn't shine. I just wasn't interested in lessons and having to continually prove myself didn't interest me either. I was artistic, though, and decided I wanted to go to Art College if I could. The nuns were less than enthusiastic at this notion and took every opportunity to tell me how I would waste my opportunities and scholarship money if I frittered away my life painting.

I wondered if those same nuns would still be saying something similar if I ended up being any good at it. Maybe if I ended up painting church ceilings would they say, "Oi! stop putting all that coloured paint up there. No-one can see it, we normally just brush on a quick bit of whitewash." Not that my painting was in any way exceptional or even outstanding, it was more the design side that interested me, but I really did enjoy painting as a hobby. Despite a distinct lack of encouragement, my mind was made up; I would try and get into art college. I applied for a place and was invited for an interview.

In the final year at school, not having to attend so many lessons and only having to revise and concentrate on the exam subjects I was taking, I now had some free time. The only rule was we had to remain on the school grounds during school hours. This gave me plenty of free time and I set about getting a portfolio of work together ready for my interview at Art college. We were also still required to do sports, and this included the weekly swimming lessons at the local swimming baths.

Although I loved swimming, I hated this particular ritual. We had to go to and from the baths in a line of twos with a teacher at the front of the line and one following up at the rear. At the age of fifteen this was an embarrassing experience. The baths were a five-minute walk from the school, surely we could have been trusted to walk there and back by ourselves. I would be glad when school was over.

Having changed back into school uniform after one particular lesson, I sat at the side of the pool waiting for my classmates so we could return to school together. Across the pool an attendant had just come on duty. He walked slowly along the edge of the pool. The swimming pool was open to the public now school lessons were over for the day. Some young women were just getting into the water, and he was talking to a few of them. I watched him for a moment inwardly laughing at the attempts he was making to chat up the girls. He was mid to late twenties, well built, with curly black hair. He seemed to know a few of the girls, and they were chatting in a good-natured way although clearly not interested in him, maybe they all had boyfriends. Unabashed he carried on chatting to them. I watched from my vantage point on the raised seating at the side of the pool and wondered if he would get lucky or not. I couldn't hear what was being said but it was clear that he was keeping them all amused with his attempts to chat them up. He turned to look at where I was sitting. Just as he turned and looked in my direction, a sudden noise from above attracted my attention away from the will-they-won't-they scene that I had been observing across the pool for the last few minutes. A strange cracking sound was filling the air, I glanced up above my head at the massive domed ceiling above us all and wondered if it was that making the noise. Then I quickly glanced across at the attendant, surely he should be doing something. At that moment a bolt of lightning came through the ceiling, tearing the roof apart with a huge rending sound, riveting me to my seat. I didn't know what was happening. I couldn't move, speak, or hear; after the initial ear-splitting noise the sudden deafening quiet sounded louder than the noise had been, I felt my eyesight was closing in around me. I thought I was going to faint. Tunnel vision centred on the lifeguard who had just come on duty, and I ceased to be aware of anything else. He was still talking to the girls as though nothing had happened. How did they not all hear that massive noise and now this strange quiet, why was nobody panicking? The roof was falling in and nobody around me seemed to be taking any notice. Just at that moment he looked up and saw me staring at him and smiled. All hope was lost, I had it and had it bad, I just didn't know what IT was. I couldn't at first understand what was happening, I must be having a dream, I would wake up at any moment at home in my own bed. But everything seemed so real, he was still there smiling at me, and I realized I was still staring at him, wondering why he wasn't doing anything.

I slowly became aware of someone shaking me. Oh, thank

goodness it was only a dream. But no, the person shaking me was one of the two nuns who had escorted the class to the swimming baths. The shaking was becoming more insistent. Sister Bernadette was convinced that I was messing about, she had apparently been speaking to me for a while, but I hadn't heard her. For my part I couldn't figure out what on earth was going on, what had happened to the roof, why was everybody behaving as though nothing had happened? I had been hit by lightning, somebody do something. I felt my arms and legs then tried to stand up, everything was working alright, maybe I was still dreaming after all. The rest of the class were ready to go and were all standing now watching and no doubt wondering what on earth I was doing. It would be hard to explain what I was doing as I had no clear idea myself. I looked across the pool, the attendant was still watching me, an amused smile on his face, then I finally realized, I smiled shyly back, no-one had ever looked at me like that before.

The rest of the class were leaving the baths, we were going back to school, every fibre of my body froze. I wanted to scream, 'No, don't make me go'. I had never felt so sick in all my life. I had to leave and didn't know if he would be there next week, or ever again. I couldn't go. Who was he? Please don't make me go. There was nothing I could do, I had to go back to school. On the way back the other girls were talking about the old man at the baths who had been showing off to all the girls. I was barely listening, I was too wrapped up in my own thoughts – "No, I hadn't seen him" – who were they talking about? I didn't really care. Then I realised who they meant. To me he was beautiful: curly dark hair, not handsome really and a bit podgy around the middle, also a lot older than me but from the second the lightning struck, none of that mattered. I was in love with him.

Revision for my O levels took a serious downturn over the next few weeks. My brain ceased to function. I sleepwalked through the days at school just waiting to see him again, hoping against hope that he would be there the following week, the waiting made worse because I couldn't talk to anyone about how I was feeling. The other girls were talking about boys they fancied; he was definitely not a boy. The following week he was on duty and the week after that it was torture to see him and not know what to do about how I was feeling. What if he had a girlfriend or even a wife? Maybe even children, what would I do then? My consolation was that each week he chatted to different women or girls and that gave me hope that he was single and looking for a girlfriend. Just thinking about spending my life without him in it made me feel sick with worry. He couldn't fail to see me looking at him and one week he said hello. Over the next few weeks, we had snatched conversations, whenever we could manage to speak without the nuns seeing what was happening. If I got changed really quickly after each swimming lesson, I could catch a few moments with him while the nuns were busy guarding the changing rooms.

My emotions were so raw at this time, I had never experienced anything like this before. I could barely speak to him, embarrassment overwhelmed me. He seemed to understand and asked if we could meet one evening. He was interested in getting to know me. So, we arranged to meet. I was in the middle of doing my exams by now so had a 9 p.m. curfew. He didn't seem to mind that I had to be in so early. After that initial meeting we started secretly going out together. I didn't tell any of my friends or the girls at school or anyone else. I seemed to have grown up overnight, they hadn't. I didn't want to explain our relationship to them or to anyone else, it was far too personal.

Jim encouraged my ambitions to go to Art College and when I had an interview and was accepted for the October term, he was really pleased for me. I didn't know if I could face leaving him, I wanted to be with him all day every day. Exams over, we had the summer before us to spend time together. I didn't have to decide straight away. Jim would have to meet my parents though; they had realized by now that I was seeing someone, I couldn't keep it a secret forever, so my mother told me to invite him for tea.

I arranged to meet Jim in town. We would drive back to my house together; I was so nervous about what my parents would have to say about the age gap, I needed moral support and thought if we arrived together, it would be easier. I had not been able to stand the thought of waiting in the house alone.

My mother had heard us talking as Jim and I were walking along the path in front of my house, and she was opening the front door as we arrived.

Jim had worn a suit for the occasion and looked very business-like. As my mother opened the door, she looked at us both then she said to me, "Where's Jim? I thought he was coming home with you." To Jim she said, "Hello, can I help you?"

"Mum, this is Jim," I said. For one of the few occasions in my life I saw my mother lost for words. Clearly Jim was not what she had expected when I told her I had a boyfriend.

Tea was a strained affair, pardon the pun, and I watched in some amusement as my mother tried to recover her composure. Jim was his usual charming self; he would win her over. I walked Jim back to his car after tea. He had found it amusing as well and said, "You obviously didn't tell your mother I was older than you."

"It doesn't matter to me that you're an old man," I said, laughing.

"But it might matter to your mum and dad. What if they stop you seeing me?" I hadn't thought about that; they would just have to get to know him better, realise we were serious about each other.

The conversation with my father was difficult; my mother had made Jim sound about ninety, the expression 'he's old enough to be your father' coming up more than once when my dad had come home that evening. Then 'he's only after one thing, he'll be off as soon as he gets it'.

Neither of them had ever told me what that one thing might be, so I feigned ignorance. Sex was never mentioned in our house, God was always listening and apparently took a dim view of such conversations and an even dimmer view of practising before you got married.

The only thing I asked my dad was, "At least meet him." He agreed to that though he wasn't happy about it.

When they did at last meet the following week, he and Jim got on really well together.

Our relationship continued through the summer. Whenever he wasn't working, we would spend time together.

My parents' worry that he would get what he wanted then disappear hadn't happened. I had willingly given him what he wanted more than once, and he was still here.

One evening towards the end of the summer, Jim was due to pick me up but hadn't arrived and there was no phone call. Unusual for him; he was late sometimes but had always called in the past. I decided to go to bed. I was upset and didn't want to listen to the endless speculations from my mother about what might have happened to delay him. I could feel undertones of 'he's got what he wanted now he's cleared off, just like we told you he would'. I didn't want to listen to any of that, I knew there had to be some good reason why he hadn't arrived or phoned.

Just after ten o'clock I heard the phone ringing. I jumped out of bed and raced to answer it.

I heard Jim say one sentence then he put the phone down. "Meet me at our usual place, I have to leave the country right now." Before my mother had a chance to realise what I was doing and try to stop me, I put a coat on over my nightclothes and ran out the door to meet him. He was on foot, dishevelled, tired, and emotional. He told me he had to leave the country and go back to Ireland. The police were after him, they had been chasing him all day. In fact, that was why he was on foot, having crashed the car earlier. I was devastated.

"What have you done?" I asked him. I was terrified of what the answer might be but if he felt he had to go immediately, it had to be something really serious.

"No time to explain," he said. He told me he loved me and would send for me as soon as he could, but he had to go. The police were right behind him.

He kissed me so tenderly I could feel the tears running down my cheeks, then he turned and walked away. I stood watching him go, fighting the urge to run after him, but sure in my heart that he wouldn't be doing this if there was any other choice. I also believed him when he said that he would send for me as soon as he could.

Still crying, I walked back to my house. As I got closer, I could hear police sirens; they were waiting for me at the house by the time I got home. The police were all over the house, searching every room, wrecking the house in the process.

My parents were in total panic. "What the hell is happening?" said my mother.

"I don't know, they are chasing Jim for some reason, that is as much as I know. He said he is going back to Ireland." I was heartbroken. The police questioning went on until the early hours of the morning, there was nothing much I could tell them. I didn't know what Jim had done or why they were after him.

Jim had been forced to leave, that was the only thing that concerned me. They wouldn't tell us why they wanted him, only that he was dangerous, and they had been after him for a while.

They put the fear of God into my parents by telling them that they would charge him with statutory rape as well because of my age. My parents were not prepared for that and were very shocked and upset, my mother in particular was petrified that I might be pregnant. Another conversation that I didn't want to have with them, especially with the police involved as well.

Eventually the questioning had to stop. I was extremely distressed, as were my parents. They would talk to me again the next day.

I cried myself to sleep that night, my entire world had just fallen apart, and I had no idea why. After only a few hours sleep, and still exhausted but calmer than I had been the night before, the police questioned me again.

They wanted a statement from me, naming all the people Jim knew, who I had met and when, and where we had met.

I was saying nothing until I knew what was going on.

They told me that Jim was involved in a lot of underground

magazines and had been writing and publishing articles. I said nothing. I knew this and couldn't see why they would be after him because of that. They were not about to tell me anything else about him and instead tried another tactic to get me to talk.

"He has lots of girlfriends. He's just using you. Now he's run off, leaving you to face the music."

True, he had left, but what they seemed to fail to realise was that before he went, he had risked being caught just to spend a few seconds saying goodbye to me. He could have just told me over the phone; why had he risked being caught? The weeks went by, and the questioning continued.

I was a prisoner in my own house; if I wanted to go out, an armed plain-clothed police officer came with me. They called it protection, said Jim was a danger to me until he was caught. Still, they wouldn't tell us why they wanted him.

The date to start college was rapidly approaching. My police escort would accompany me there as well. I was only fifteen so still classed as a child. If I didn't agree to the escort, they would take me into care, and I wouldn't be able to start college. I had set my heart on going to college so had to agree and at least the police escort to and from the college each day saved me having to take several buses each way.

My escort would drop me off first thing in the morning then sometimes hang around college, sometimes leave and come back later – it varied each day. At least I knew I would only have to put up with this for a few weeks. Once I turned sixteen the threat of putting me in care would be over.

It was difficult to have a normal time at college, hard to explain away my escort and the fact that I could never stay late after lessons, so I just sat tight until my birthday and then threatened them with legal action unless they withdrew my escort.

They had no option but to do as I wanted.

I threw myself into college life with gusto and enjoyed every minute of my new freedom. After life at school which had been only girls, I found myself surrounded by men and I loved it. It was fantastic to be in an environment where art was thought of as worthwhile. I was missing Jim so much it helped to keep my mind occupied while I waited for him to get in contact. I never doubted that he would get in touch regardless of what everyone else thought.

I knew him, they didn't. It was just a matter of time.

One lunchtime a man sat next to me in the college cafeteria. He was drinking coffee and with the cup held in front of his mouth so that people couldn't see he was speaking to me, he said, "Jim sent me. Meet me outside in ten minutes." Then he got up and walked away. I went upstairs and got my coat and bag and ten minutes later went outside. I had only taken a few steps when I heard a shout.

"Armed Police. Put your hands above your head!"

An armed policeman had run towards me, pointing a handgun in my direction.

Police appeared everywhere; I was handcuffed and shoved into a police car.

The questioning started again. I told them exactly what had happened, I had done nothing wrong. Why were they holding me?

They said Jim was a wanted man, I was consorting with him. If only.

They had to let me go. The man who had spoken to me in the cafeteria had gotten away, there was nothing they could hold me on.

I went back to college the following day. No hiding what was going on now, too many people had seen the police the previous day. The notoriety and interest lasted a few weeks then it was yesterday's news and I started to make a few friends. There was still no word from Jim. Months slowly went by. The hours spent travelling to and from college, now that I had to take buses, were taking a toll on me and I decided to look for a flat nearer to the college.

In the end I couldn't afford a flat so ended up in a shared house, sharing a bedroom with Jane, a friend from college. I had spent the last five years surrounded by nuns and had no intention of becoming one; so, free from all the restrictions that had been holding me back for so long, and a new friend to do things with, we broke loose and enjoyed ourselves.

Life in college was everything I had hoped it would be I loved the student life. Dating different men was an eye opener though. I had assumed that having done the deed with Jim I now knew what the sex thing was all about and had thought that experiences would be pretty much the same, just a different person to do it with. How wrong I was and what a disappointment it turned out to be, especially the first one. When it was all over, at least from his point of view, he had looked so pleased with himself, I had looked at him with a 'what the hell was that supposed to be' expression. When he then also appeared to think that was definitely the end of it and he had done a fine job, I had found it hard to hide my astonishment. I did my best to hide my disappointment and thought maybe it was just nerves on his part and it would get better, but it didn't, and even gentle hints from me were ignored; he thought he was an expert. I was just supposed to lay there and look grateful apparently, oh well, just have to try another, they couldn't all be this bad.

The months passed, Christmas came and went and still I heard nothing from Jim. I missed him but knew that it might be some time before we could be together. After what had happened the last time, he would have to be even more careful next time. What I had no way of knowing was that he had already been arrested and imprisoned in Belfast and that he had then escaped and was on the run again.

One bright sunny afternoon I was in the studio catching up on some work, it was one of the first bright days of spring. After a long, cold winter, the promise of a warm spring and then hopefully a hot summer was in the air. I had my back to the door concentrating on a piece of work that I was supposed to be handing in later that afternoon, the rest of the room was quiet as well, everyone focusing on the work at hand. Without fully realizing why, I had become aware of someone moving towards me across the room. There were only a few people in the studio, all at the other end of the room, whoever it was was clearly heading towards me. I resisted the urge to turn around. I had one small bit of work to finish, I would do that before I turned. A strange sensation had begun to distract me from the job at hand, the hairs on my arms were standing on end and an odd feeling now moved up and down my spine. I remained still, aware of someone now standing right behind me. I couldn't decide if I was terrified or unbelievably excited. A female voice quietly said, "Do you want to be with Jim?"

I said, "Yes."

"OK, follow me," the voice said.

I turned to face a young woman only a few years older than me with short dark hair cut to curl around her face. She was very attractive with an Audrey Hepburn look about her. I put down the piece that I had been working on and without further conversation I allowed her to lead me out of the studio, down the stairs, and then out of the building. Neither of us spoke on the way out, there was nothing more to say really, I trusted that Jim had sent her and that she would take me to him.

As we exited into the bright sunshine a moment of panic gripped me, what if the Police were here again? They could arrest her, and she would be in serious trouble. She seemed perfectly calm and that to some extent reassured me. The fact still remained though, I was about to do something momentous that would change my entire life – there would be no going back. Was I really ready for this, whatever this might be?

I half expected there to be that warning shout like last time, and I tensed, waiting for the police to descend on us, but absolutely nothing happened, normal life carried on all around us. We calmly walked away from college, got on a bus, and went back to my house. At the house I packed a small carrier bag with a few bits and pieces, knowing I could not risk taking more in case anyone realized what was happening and tried to stop us. I wished we could have waited at the house for a few hours till Jane got home, I didn't want to leave without saying goodbye, but it was too big a risk. The further away we could get before anyone realized I was missing the safer it would be. I had met Jane on my first day at college and we had become firm friends. She was on the same course as me and when I had decided to move out of home and look for somewhere to live closer to college, Jane had decided to move too and we now shared the house with three other girls. We spent most of our free time together and, looking at what I was now about to do, I had pangs of guilt about the way I was going to leave and wished it could be different. I had no idea whether I would ever see her again. We had shared some fantastic times together, I would really miss Jane.

I had written a note for my parents and also one for Jane.

I had asked Jane to give the note to my parents when they realized I had gone.

Then, with one final look around, I walked away from everything that I had up until now known as my life and leaving it all behind me I headed into an unknown future. If I felt frightened it was quickly overtaken by a sense of fantastic excitement, realizing that in a few hours, after all the waiting, I would finally be with Jim again.

CHAPTER 4

Kilcoole

The flight back to Ireland had been uneventful. After only my second plane journey, I was feeling like an old hand at this, even the passport issue no longer seemed like the problem I had feared it might be those few weeks before.

Now on this daytime flight and viewing Paris from the air and marvelling at all the new sights and at England with all the old familiar sights, albeit viewed from a different angle, I was beginning to feel optimistic that Ireland could really become a new home for me. Having landed and exited the airport safely we headed for the car park.

We collected the car and set off for our new home. The excitement I had been feeling about the new house was beginning to abate a little and a few realities were starting to rear their ugly heads. Our happy homecoming also meant a return to all the old problems that we had managed to leave behind for the last few precious weeks and my thoughts were also tinged with dread at the prospect of having to deal with Jim's family, or rather one particular brother plus fiancé.

I hoped that we might get at least a few days peace to

settle in before any of them descended on us. So far, I had only met two brothers, one of whom had been ok. There were several more to go, plus his sisters, plus assorted in-laws, and last but not least his mother. I did not imagine for one minute that she would welcome me with open arms; a British girlfriend, they would be keeping quiet about that in Belfast. I did hope though that she would at least give me a fair chance. My only saving grace, if I could claim it as such, was I had at least been raised a Catholic.

As we drove past the turn off for Bray, I wondered what the gruesome twosome were doing right now and if they had any regrets about the manner of our departure, probably not, I decided. If Jim was thinking about it at all he made no comment.

We arrived at Kilcoole, the small collection of houses too little to be called a village, more a hamlet, and turned down the narrow lane that led to the house that was to be our new home. A small shop marked the corner, otherwise you could easily miss it. I would have to pay attention now, if Jim was away at all it would be handy to know where the house was exactly secreted away as it was in this maze of country lanes. I was used to town streets with names on the corner that ran in relatively straight lines with people about to ask directions, this place was deserted.

The lane seemed longer than I remembered but, just as I was beginning to think Jim had taken a wrong turn, the house came into view and along with it the smell of the sea came wafting through the open car window. We were here.

The house was more or less as I remembered from my previous fleeting view; what I hadn't noticed before was just how big the garden to the front of the house was and then I spotted the several outbuildings to the rear of the house almost hidden by an overgrown hedge. Jim opened the five-bar gate and drove in, parking in front of the house and turning the engine off.

For several moments we both remained seated in the car looking at the house. This was serious now, once we walked through that door our lives would be altered forever, different in so many ways from the existence we had shared at Bray, no longer just girlfriend and boyfriend sharing fleeting moments alone in other people's homes or hotels but a committed couple living together in a shared home. Even in Paris it had still seemed so unreal, as though I would wake up at any moment and still be in my old life.

If we had been arrested at any point before this I would have been shipped off back home, a victim in everything and therefore presumed innocent, but setting up home together made me complicit in Jim's life and forever guilty.

We both slowly got out of the car and stood on the front doorstep, while Jim put the key in the lock I looked around at the garden and driveway. I had never imagined myself living in a house with its own driveway.

Door open, we still hesitated. Jim slowly took me in his arms and kissed me very gently on my left cheek then just as gently whispered in my ear (I love you) my legs were giving way as I whispered back (carry me). My eyes closed he carried me into the house and upstairs. I would have to look at the rest of the house later, right now I didn't care what it looked like, I was just so glad to be finally here and with Jim.

Some hours later, back downstairs again, we collected our things from the car, and I took a look at our new home. It felt so good to finally think of somewhere as home.

The front door opened onto a small hallway, on the left were two doors, on the right only one, and immediately in front at the end of the hallway was the bathroom.

The first left-hand door was a dining room – good, there was a telephone Jim would be able to contact me when he was away. The next door on the left was a small bedroom, the single door on the right was the sitting room. You had to walk through the sitting room to get to the kitchen which wrapped itself around the back of the house and overlooked a small, cobbled courtyard which in turn led to the outbuildings, they were maybe stables but I would take a look later when I had some more clothes on. The bedrooms upstairs were accessed via a staircase off the kitchen and took their positions, one over the sitting room, one over the dining room, both with views over the front garden to the sea beyond.

It was going to be a bit of a trek to the bathroom if you needed to go in the middle of the night.

The house was neat and clean but very old fashioned, we spread out the few things that I had bought in Dublin and unpacked our suitcases into the bedroom wardrobe and drawers. We had stopped on the way from the airport to pick up a few groceries so while I made a fry-up Jim made some phone calls. After eating we took a walk to the beach and watched the sun go down before walking back to the house. Was it now home and would we be able to enjoy it in peace? I hoped so.

The next few weeks passed in an almost dream state, we were both so happy, we ate and slept when we felt like it, dressing or more often not dressing as the mood took us, only occasionally venturing out when hunger got the better of us and we needed to get in some supplies. Life was idyllic but we both knew it couldn't last like this. The honeymoon had to end sometime.

His family would find out soon enough that we were back, and our peace would be shattered. We would make the most of it while we had the chance.

Halfway through the third week the phone started ringing, the shrill noise echoed through the entire house, making us both jump. Jim answered it in a few short sentences, saying, "Don't talk on the phone I'll, call you back," then he got some change and went out to the phone box. I would very quickly grow to hate these phone calls, they always signalled trouble. If Jim thought the conversation couldn't be had over our landline, then it was serious.

The house was so lonely when he was out of it, I would wander from room to room looking at all the things that reminded me of him, anything he had touched or worn of particular interest. I pined when he wasn't around, a pain very physical starting in my stomach, making me feel like vomiting then spreading upwards, pulsing through my head until I felt as though it would explode if he didn't get back soon. The nights he had to be away were always the worst, never knowing for sure how long he would be away or what time of day or night he would be back. I didn't want to leave the house in case he got back while I was out, and I missed a few precious moments with him.

The fear of what if he never made it back was always playing on my mind. I knew that what he was doing could get him killed and that knowledge paralyzed me when he wasn't around. I needed him to be where I could see him and know that he was safe.

Each time he got back we would have a few hours, sometimes even a day or two before the phone would find him again and people would start arriving at the house.

Apart from his relatives he was forever picking up waifs and strays along the way, people naturally gravitated towards Jim.

Strangers stayed at the house, sometimes days, sometimes weeks. The interesting ones usually moved on more quickly, they had places to go, people to see, new experiences to encounter to keep them interested, only the boring ones hung around long after they had outstayed their initial welcome. Jim brought home a hippy couple one evening, hippies hadn't really made an impact on Ireland yet, it would be interesting to see what Ireland would think of them. These two had been hitch hiking and he had picked them up. Ever hungry for new experiences, Jim was fascinated to know all about their lifestyle, they were happy to tell it endlessly, the 'cool, man' expression however got very boring very quickly. The subtle suggestion from me that their time with us was over passed them both by, or, they simply chose to ignore it altogether.

Jim had been away for a few days and when he got back it was time for action, I wanted them out of the house and the sooner the better. Their endless tales of the hippy idyll had annoyed me; it sounded plausible on the surface, a heaven on earth, but as every true believer will tell you, attaining heaven required hours spent on your knees earning your place in the Promised Land.

These two did nothing to earn theirs, they took from the moment they entered the house, never once thinking that maybe they could lend a hand, tidy up, wash a few of the dishes that they had used or wash themselves even. Our home was being treated like a guest house and this landlady had had enough. They on the other hand seemed to be happy to live with the smell of their unwashed bodies and clothes. All of this I could have possibly overlooked been benign but the final straw that broke this camel's back had been when they moved their mattress onto the floor, blocking the bedroom door permanently open. They were in the small bedroom next to the bathroom, and it had now gotten to the point where you couldn't go to the bathroom without witnessing a live sex show from these two.

Thanks, but no thanks.

Jim did see my point. He had invited some friends round the previous week for the evening and hippy girl had sat on the floor for the whole evening cross legged with no underwear on. The frequently exposed breasts were one thing, this was something else altogether. It had been hard to hold a conversation under those circumstances. Our friends had left early, we were in Ireland after all, things were very different here.

Not having taken the many hints from me, Jim now spoke to them more directly. He gave them some money and a lift into Dublin, we were rid of them at last.

While he was gone, I put the room back together and put the sheets in the washing machine, I did debate just throwing them away but that seemed so wasteful. In the end a good soak in bleach seemed to do the trick.

I pleaded with Jim, "please don't bring any more weirdos home." He promised to try not to, but I wasn't holding my breath on that one, though he just didn't seem to be able to help himself.

We had been going through a few tough weeks, nerves were frayed all around, everyone jumpy. Jim had been up and down to Belfast on numerous occasions, the phone was going all hours of the day and night, we were worn out.

I hadn't seen Jim alone for what seemed like months. I was missing my private time with him. Whenever we did manage to get time alone, I seemed to be complaining all the time, spoiling the little time we did have.

He complained that I didn't deal with enough things myself, preferring to leave it for him to deal with. I was still unsure of myself in these new surroundings, never quite believing that this was truly my home, and I could decide what happened here, especially when it concerned his family. It all came to a head one Sunday afternoon.

We were alone for once. I had made some cheese, bread, salad, and pickles for lunch and had laid it out between us on the coffee table in the sitting room. The argument we were having was so trivial that it should have been over in seconds. I had always previously backed down.

Today though I had had enough.

Jim was goading me, really pushing me to let it all out, knowing me as well as he did, he knew exactly which buttons to press. Often, he tried to encourage me to let myself go more, not be so repressed, but years of conditioning to be meek and uncomplaining had had a huge effect on me and was not easy to shake off.

Since I had been here with him, I had taken a long hard look at the relationships around me, those from my childhood, and now those in Ireland, how else were you supposed to learn the art of being with someone else for the rest of your life other than by learning from what you had experienced?

So far, all the Irish relationships I had seen had the men firmly in command, just backed up by the extra layers of religion.

At least between Jim and me it wasn't like that; he had always encouraged me to be my own person, but what if we married, would things change then?

As a child, repression seemed to be the order of the day although I hadn't really understood what had been happening to me, that had just been how life was, you did as you were told, even more so if you were a girl. All relationships that I had known had been underpinned by religion, that put men clearly in charge, even down to the wedding vows stating that the wife should love, honour, and obey etc. I had always known that I wanted to be a mother, never sure that I wanted to be a wife though. Maybe it was the whole obey thing I had never been happy about, and the idea that a man would decide what I could or couldn't do once I was an adult. I had had more than enough of that as a child. Maybe there was a seed of rebellion in me after all.

Well, if Jim wanted to see self-expression, letting go etc., he was going to see it today. I had had enough.

We were still talking back and forth, Jim trying his best to get under my skin, I had seen him do it to other people, manoeuvring and making them squirm until he went for the jugular with a lightening retort. I was quicker with the one liners than he was, something he had admired in me from the start, so was easily holding my own against his comments, sparring back and forth, enjoying it at first but then growing bored.

It was at this bored moment that I lost my concentration,

and I said the fatal line:

"If you don't stop annoying me, I'm going to throw something at you."

He grinned, he had me now and he knew it. I had to go through with my threat no matter what.

Then he said, "I dare you." The final straw.

I picked up the nearest thing to me on the table, the bottle of pickles, and holding it in my hand I raised my arm as though to throw it.

I never knew beforehand whether or not I would have actually thrown the jar but when Jim saw my arm raised, he was sure I wouldn't, and he started laughing at me.

Bad mistake.

I warned him once to stop laughing, he didn't, so I threw it.

He ducked just in time, the jar missed him by inches, his laugh stopping in mid breath as the jar smashed against the wall and little brown blobs of pickle began sliding down the wallpaper.

It surprised the both of us.

All would have been well if Jim had just let it go at that, but surveying the wall he said, "You're going to have to clear that up now or the stain will never come off."

I screamed, "Don't tell me what to do, ever!"

That comment was unfair on my part, which, if I had been rational at the time, I would have completely acknowledged.

Jim had never told me what to do, even though he was fourteen years older than me and was used to bossing around his brothers and sisters, amongst others.

I at that moment though was not rational. He looked at me, wondering what on earth he had unleashed. I was thinking about the absurdity of the situation we were now in.

There were many people who idolized Jim for who he was and the cause he was fighting for, there were also as many people if not more who were frightened of him for exactly the same reasons.

I wondered how many of them would consider throwing things at him under any circumstances.

We had reached a watershed moment; if he had taken his second chance that afternoon and let it go it would have been over. Instead he said, "Stop now," and went to catch my arm. It might have been to cuddle me and end the argument, I didn't see it that way though or even consider the possibility and instead of waiting to see picked up something else from the table and threw it at him. He stood up and backed away straight into the corner of the room. The last object I had thrown, I realized, was the bread and it had missed him. Now I was really mad.

He laughed again.

Somewhere deep inside me, a place I couldn't remember going to before, a dam broke, all the hard and painful things that I had hidden for so many years were hiding in that dark place just waiting for their chance to explode into the light and wreak havoc on me all over again. The fact that I didn't properly remember putting them there only made it worse. I had blocked out too many things, the space was full now, I needed to let some of it out.

Like a large boil, so much better when it finally bursts. Still hearing him laughing, I was now acutely aware of a reduction in my vision. I had heard the expression red mist now, I was experiencing it for myself.

The room was swimming all around me, the red mist descending now as I grabbed another object from the coffee table in passing as I jumped over it and aimed a blow at Jim. I had been hit so many times as a child but had never imagined that I would ever resort to hitting anyone myself, let alone someone I loved. As he moved to one side my hand connected with his body.

I felt a huge jolt to my right arm, there had been something in my hand, it had hit the wall first and with such force that not only my arm but my whole shoulder took the impact and I fell backwards, sitting down first onto the coffee table then falling in a heap on the floor.

The laughing had stopped, I sat on the floor dazed for a few moments, still seeing red all around me. Then one by one colours started to return. I looked at my pearlized pale blue shoes, I loved those shoes, and then at the rug, all the colours pretty normal again, then came the dawning realization that Jim was not making any sound.

I looked up, he was standing where I had left him, his face

a bit pale, a look of concern on his face but he was still not moving or saying anything.

I had given him two chances that afternoon, maybe he had learned his lesson and was waiting for me to say something or to make the first move.

I glanced down and saw he was holding his left side, maybe I had hit him harder than I had realized, then I saw the bread knife sticking in the wall and the small red patch on his shirt.

It was only a flesh wound really but he was still pinned to the wall by his shirt. I looked at him for a moment and thought about saying 'don't laugh at me again' but I thought he had probably gotten the point in more ways than one that afternoon.

We cleared away the broken remnants of our lunch and I patched up his side.

Later that day the consequences of what could have happened hit me like a sledgehammer.

If Jim hadn't moved when he did, the knife would have gone straight into his stomach. I couldn't believe that I had so much violence in me, I could have killed him in one moment of madness, the thought of it left me shaking uncontrollably. We talked long into the night about the dark place that I had been to and the secrets that I had buried away there. Talking was slowly leeching out more of the forgotten secrets until by morning I felt nearly depleted, the memories no longer forgotten and buried, I could deal with them now.

My 18th birthday was coming up and we had been away a lot the last few months, in and out of hotels most of the time, I just wanted some quiet time at home with Jim. While we had been away, Jim's brother Elmo and Elmo's wife Patricia, plus assorted children, had moved into our house at Kilcoole so I wasn't certain exactly how peaceful it would be, but I just wanted to stop travelling for a few weeks. Jim had said we could do whatever I wanted for my birthday but of all the choices on offer I had decided to have a quiet meal at home rather than go out, steak always on the menu for Jim even though I wasn't that good at cooking it.

We invited some old friends, John and Gerri, to spend the evening with us, I always enjoyed their company, and Jim's brother Elmo and his wife Patricia.

The meal ended up being pretty good, even the steak was better than usual. After dinner Jim gave me my birthday present – a ring box.

He had proposed to me some weeks ago on one magical night in Nice at a restaurant overlooking the sea. The usually ebullient Jim on that night had seemed almost shy, clearly something was on his mind. We had ordered starters and when they arrived, he had looked at me several times as though unsure what to do or say. "What's the matter?" I asked. I had been worried; he had looked so strange. He had taken my hand, got down on one knee, told me he loved me, and then asked me to marry him. I was stunned. It almost crossed my mind that he was joking but I looked into his eyes and knew that he had never been more serious. To a round of applause from the other diners I had said "yes".

We hadn't told anyone that we were engaged but now the secret was out.

I looked down at my ring, it was beautiful, a perfect diamond set in four pillars of white gold. I couldn't take my eyes of it. Jim said, "Aren't you going to put it on?"

But I didn't want to wear it yet. I said instead, "Let's organize a proper engagement party and then everyone can see it together." Jim hadn't really thought about how he was going to tell the rest of his family but a party would be good. The others were sworn to secrecy until the party. I went to bed happy that night, it was the best birthday I had ever had.

As many of Jim's family that could make it and a few good friends were invited for the following weekend to my birthday/surprise engagement party.

I had spent most of the week getting food and drink in and most of the actual day cooking and getting stuff ready for the evening, hopefully it should be a good do.

We had even invited the gruesome twosome, they were his family, we would just have to try and get along. The last time I had seen them had been at their wedding in Belfast. Jim and I had gone to his mother's house and then to the church but hadn't attended the reception. Jim was so well known now that we couldn't have risked staying around for too long, word would have gotten out, we didn't want to risk Jim getting caught and ruining their big day.

My birthday party was going well, even the new Mr and Mrs Gruesome Twosome seemed in good spirits. Once all the children were settled to sleep in our spare room, the party really got going and at the stroke of midnight Jim made the announcement that he and I were officially engaged, and this was also our engagement party. Everyone wanted to talk about plans for our wedding, where we would settle after we were married etc. but we hadn't really decided anything yet. We were happy just catching up on everyone else's news. I hadn't been wearing my engagement ring, wanting to wait until everyone was together to show them, so Jim went upstairs to fetch it.

Conversation was quieter now, there was always a drop in volume whenever Jim left a room.

Sean, who was across the coffee table from me and had been drinking quite heavily all evening, suddenly said, "Did you get our wedding photos developed yet?" The question surprised me, I had only taken a few snapshots at his mother's house and some at the church before and after their wedding service, I didn't know why he was showing any interest. Photography was a hobby of mine from college days, but Sean had never been interested before. I hadn't used up all the film yet, plus to get it developed I had to go into Dublin, and we had been away so much that I hadn't been there since their wedding.

I glanced across at him and replied, "No, I haven't had a chance to get the film developed yet." I barely got to the end of my sentence before the coffee table in front of me lurched in my direction and a cascade of glasses, plates, and food hit my lap, showering me in broken glass.

I stood up gingerly, letting the food and glass trickle off my skirt into a disgusting pile on the carpet in front of me. The initial shock of thinking that the table had been upset by accident was quickly overtaken by the realization that Sean had tipped it up deliberately and had then proceeded to smash a bottle against the edge of it.

The same bottle he was now holding at my throat.

Silence had descended over all our guests, everyone now aware of what was happening, all eyes on me, not quite the attention I had wanted on our special night.

I realized that Sean was by now completely out of control and he had started ranting, mainly about why hadn't I had time to get the film developed I had f— all to do all day, etc. etc. Then followed a tirade of insults, mainly about my Nationality and that I was a bitch. I tried to remain as calm as possible, now acutely aware that I was in the very same corner that Jim had stood in when I lunged at him. I knew there was no escape.

As the seconds ticked by, all the possible outcomes began to go through my mind.

Jim would be back soon. Sean might calm down before then, not likely though.

What the hell would Jim do when he saw what was happening?

I just hoped nobody tried to jump Sean, the room wasn't

that big and was crowded, someone was bound to get hurt if not by Sean, then by all the broken glass on the floor.

Elmo was doing his best to calm the situation, talking very quietly to Sean, trying to reason with him, but Sean was having none of it. The broken bottle still held to my throat, he continued screaming at me with his list of supposed injustices that I had perpetrated against him but as usual it mainly boiled down to me being British.

How could his brother betray the Cause by fraternizing with the enemy?

I had been keeping a close eye on Sean, if he lunged at me then I was going to at least attempt to get out of the way. Jim had heard the screaming and came downstairs, now entering the room behind Sean but still able to see clearly what was happening. Sean heard him and turned; Jim ducked in time to miss the bottle still in Sean's hand at the same time landing a good punch on the side of his head. Sean staggered backwards, slipping on the spilled food. Jim moved around the upturned table towards me to check I was ok. Sean took his opportunity to leg it out of the sitting room and then out the front door, still yelling insults about me as he went.

Jim had seen and heard enough. He turned and ran after Sean who was now somewhere in the garden. Pandemonium broke out, everyone trying to get out of the front door at the same time, some shouting to Sean, some to Jim. I was the furthest from the sitting room door and still in considerable shock so waited for the melee to die down a little before attempting to go after Jim.

I just remember shouting to everyone, "Mind the broken glass."

Out in the garden the party guests were split into several groups all searching the bushes and trees, it was obvious that Sean was no longer in the garden and people were already spilling onto the lane and into the fields around the house looking for him. I was distraught, all the effort that had gone into this, it was supposed to be so special and was now ruined over what? I still had no idea.

I went back indoors. I just wanted to go to my bedroom and try to forget the whole thing. As I walked back through the front door and into the hallway, I noticed that the dining room door was open.

Jim usually kept it closed, he used it as an office, nobody except me was allowed in there without his say so, especially when the children were around as Jim also kept his harpoon gun in there. The thought struck me maybe Sean had sneaked back into the house and was hiding in there, at least he was minus bottle now.

Gingerly, I eased the door further open and moved my hand along the wall to flick on the light switch. The room was empty, I checked behind the door, there was no one there but there was something different, the harpoon gun, normally on a high shelf, was missing. I realized that Sean had not had time to get it when he ran out of the house, Jim must have it. My heart nearly stopped; even though I didn't like Sean, I didn't want to see him with a two-foot-long spear embedded in him and I knew that Jim was so mad anything was possible. I ran back outside to find Elmo, of all of them he was the most sensible and needed to know that Jim had the harpoon gun with him.

It had suddenly gone from an almost amusing drunken escapade that would have ended in a brawl, only a few bruises and black eyes to worry about the next day, to something far more serious. Sean had insulted me in Jim's home and in front of people that mattered to Jim, I was now really frightened that Jim might do him some serious harm.

Reputation was at stake here. Jim would have to be seen to deal with this. It was like being involved with the Mafia, reputation was everything and had to be guarded fiercely. I found Elmo heading back to the house, he had found Sean and had already bundled him and Oonagh into a car to be driven home by one of the few people still sober enough to drive, I was so relieved I started crying.

Jim was still running around somewhere outside, we could hear occasional shouts but decided to leave him to his shouting, he would run out of steam soon enough. By the time Jim eventually got back to the house I was up in the bedroom surrounded by the women all giving me advice about how I should handle the situation, the only thing I could see was a wrecked house and a wrecked engagement party and still no idea why.

Everyone was upset, it had frightened them seeing the

bottle at my face, they were all wondering how I managed to stay so calm. I thought it best not to enlighten them about my argument with Jim a few months before.

The slamming front door told us of Jim's return minutes before he got to the bedroom, I knew there was no way he had got to Sean, they didn't. I didn't want Jim to know of Elmo's involvement in getting Sean away from the house, that could wait until the morning when he had calmed down, so I looked as surprised as the rest of them when he told us all that Sean was nowhere to be found.

They all breathed a sigh of relief.

Jim, still mad and having not found anyone to take it out on, decided to try yelling at me instead. I must have done something to upset Sean, etc. etc. I remained calm and just repeated exactly what had happened, still saying, "I have no idea why he was so upset." Half of Jim's female relatives were in the bedroom at this point all agreeing with my version of events, even if he didn't believe me, he knew after all how much I disliked Sean, he couldn't argue with all of them.

They all calmed Jim down, I was too emotionally drained to be bothered telling the story more than once and I fell asleep.

Some people went home, some stayed the night sleeping in armchairs or on the floor, wherever there was any space. Some spent the night scattered around the garden and surrounding fields, a few even made it as far as the beach and slept there.

I didn't sleep long and as soon as daylight was coming through our bedroom window, I was up making breakfast and cleaning up the mess as best I could around sleeping bodies.

Jim eventually woke mid-morning and came down to eat, he joined the throng of people in the house who had been keeping me busy since dawn cooking fried breakfasts. Now hopefully for the explanation about what the hell had been wrong with Sean the previous evening.

Jim proceeded to tell us all that the photographer the gruesome twosome had hired to photograph their wedding had messed up big time and they didn't have a single decent picture of their wedding. The only other person that they knew had a camera and had taken a lot of pictures was me. Well, it wasn't my fault they had hired a rubbish photographer, if they had bothered to tell me about it I would have had my films developed for them. Sean had spoken to Jim apparently and had asked him to speak to me about the photos I had taken. Jim had just forgotten.

Once again, not my fault. I knew nothing about it but was getting the blame anyway.

I said to Jim and the assembled company who were now all discussing the situation, "If Sean had just asked me a civil question when they first arrived then I would have told him I didn't know about it, and it would have been sorted there and then. Instead, he just assumed that it was all my fault and waited till he was drunk and Jim was out of the room before having a go at me." Most of the crowd were on my side, even the members of his family who would usually be expected to side with Sean were showing some sympathy for my situation.

I finished cooking the last breakfast then I went and got my camera and gave the films to Jim and just said, "You get them developed and give them to them. I don't want anything to do with either of them again. I don't want to see or speak to them or for them to come to the house and if I keep these films, I might well be tempted to destroy them."

Jim tried one last time to protest Sean had been drunk etc. "I don't care. I haven't ever done anything to either of them. I am not going to put up with threats and insults in my own house," I said. "Last night, if you had gotten hold of him, what would you have done to him?"

No answer to that one.

It took several weeks for things to really die down after our engagement fiasco but, true to his word, Jim had told Sean never to darken our doorstep again.

We would still meet at family things away from our house, there was no real avoiding that, I didn't want to put a rift in the family and make people choose sides, so we would go along to any events and just avoid those two as much as possible.

Jim had had my films developed and apparently some of the photos had been quite good so at least they had a record of their big day.

Life gained a certain normality for a short time. We would walk on the beach most days, go out to lunch or go and have dinner with friends.

On the days we stayed at home I would cook. I was getting reasonably good now and we would often have people come to our house for dinner. Jim had slowly started to talk about what he had been up to while we had been apart. I didn't really understand what had triggered the whole conflict that seemed to have been going on most of my lifetime, so I had started studying Irish history. I read as much as I could and spoke to his friends about it. He would never go into any great detail about what he was actually doing, and I worried that maybe he didn't trust me, but he reassured me that he trusted me completely; it was for my own safety that he kept some things from me, saying that what I knew would be a danger to me, not what I didn't know.

We had friends to stay one weekend and after a very late Sunday night, they departed, leaving Jim and me just a little on the drunk side of sober.

I had fallen into bed knackered; clearing up could wait until tomorrow.

I avoided opening my eyes the next day, my head hurt. If I pretended to be asleep for long enough maybe Jim would wake up and go and make the breakfast. I wanted to eat something, just didn't fancy smelling it while it cooked.

I lay in bed half dreaming of a bacon sandwich. I was sure I could smell bacon cooking; that and a nice cup of tea would do me just now.

I realised that I could actually smell bacon. Jim must

already be up. My normal enthusiasm for getting up early had completely deserted me this particular morning and the headache that had been in the front of my head when I had first been aware that I was awake had now spread to the rest of my head and was now moving down my neck and into my back. I needed painkillers and fast. I had two options; I could wait for Jim to come upstairs, and he could get them for me although that might take a while because he was cooking our breakfast, or I could go to the bathroom and fetch them myself. Very gingerly I opened one eye as slowly as possible and tried to focus on the ceiling. The light from the window seemed to be so much brighter than usual this morning.

Oh no, I was hallucinating. I could see myself floating on the ceiling, was this really what a hangover was like? One question kept coming into my mind, when it could find a space around the pain which was now a throbbing sensation, making me feel like vomiting.

"Why was I dressed in a bikini?" I closed my eye and tried opening the other one instead.

It was even worse. The hallucination was still looking at me. I did look pretty good though.

Both eyes closed, I lay thinking about what to do. If I lay really still, I felt OK, no headache, no sick feeling, so why was I seeing things? I slid my hand across the bed. Jim was definitely not there, and I could still smell bacon. I could just lie here with my eyes closed until he came back. Eventually, after what had seemed like an age, I heard him coming up the stairs into the bedroom, then the sound of a tray being placed on the bedside table.

He said, "Stop trying to pretend you're still asleep. I've made the breakfast." He knew me so well.

"I can't open my eyes," I said.

"Why not? I wanted you to see the surprise I've got for you."

"I can't think about surprises right now. Every time I open my eyes I hallucinate."

"What?"

So, I told him, "Every time I open my eyes, I see myself floating on the ceiling, dressed in a bikini." I had hoped for a bit of sympathy, instead I got uproarious laughter. "Thanks very much," I said.

He said, "Open your eyes."

"No." Then he said, "Is the hallucination holding the spear gun that I chased Sean with, and do you have a fish knife strapped to your thigh?"

"I don't know, I didn't look properly. How do you know what it looks like anyway?"

He held my hand and said, "It's OK, honestly, open your eyes and look at the surprise I did for you." I opened both eyes, looked at him, and then sneaked a peek at the ceiling.

It took me a moment to comprehend what I was actually seeing. I was indeed on the ceiling and in a bikini with a spear gun in one hand and a fish knife strapped to my thigh.

Over our cup of tea and bacon sandwiches, he told me he had taken the photograph while we had been in Corsica and had liked it so much, he had had it blown up to life-size, and last night after I fell asleep, he had glued it to the ceiling.

I had no idea he had taken the photograph, even less idea how he had managed to glue it to the ceiling above our bed without waking me up. He enjoyed looking at his handiwork, apart from the fact that he liked the photograph so much, telling me I looked beautiful, he enjoyed my reaction to it as well. After the initial shock I did like the photo. Previously I had never liked having my photograph taken. It was weird, though, to wake up each morning and see myself on the ceiling, so after a few weeks I took it down.

Jim was spending more time in Belfast, sometimes several days at a time. I missed him but at least we could keep in touch by phone.

He rang one afternoon, saying he would be home that evening.

Good, my chance to surprise him. I had been shopping in Dublin and bought some new underwear. I would try and remember some of the moves I had seen at the nightclub in Paris and see what he thought. I had plenty of time to get ready; he wouldn't be home till after dark so I took a bath and got dressed, or undressed I should say, and waited for him, setting the mood by lighting scented candles around the house and putting on some mood music.

Hearing the car pull into the driveway, I ran and opened the front door. Momentarily blinded by the car's headlights, I forgot what I was supposed to be doing and stood for a second, then thought, *quick, look sexy.*

I stood holding the front door, stroking it in what I hoped was a seductive manner. Well, I hoped Jim thought it was seductive, not just that I had run out in my underwear to polish the doorknob. He was surprised all right, so was his passenger. I shrieked, ran back into the house and hid upstairs. I was so embarrassed. He followed me upstairs.

"You never told me you were bringing anyone back with you," I said.

"I didn't know until the last minute. Anyway, you've never opened the door in your underwear before." Never likely to again either after tonight.

"Who is he anyway?"

"It's Howard Marks. You've spoken to him on the phone loads of times." That didn't make it any easier to go back downstairs. I had indeed spoken to Howard on many occasions but had never expected to meet him. Jim had always kept business away from our home. Howard had appeared on the scene some time ago and had quickly struck up a friendship with Jim. I was wary of this sudden acquaintance; too many people we didn't know were becoming involved in our lives. I didn't trust them and felt they were a danger to us. Jim liked Howard and thought I was getting paranoid. I had told him I was being followed when I was in Holland. He thought I was imagining it.

I knew I wasn't.

I had gone shopping to the local town the last time I had been in Holland and spent a few hours browsing in dress shops. The entire time the hairs on the back of my neck had been standing on end. I knew beyond a shadow of a doubt that someone was following me. During that same evening I had gone out for a drink and to get some dinner at the nightclub that was in the same block as our flat. During the evening a man approached me at the bar and tried to strike up a conversation. He tried very hard to appear casual. I just knew he was a policeman. I had spent enough time around the police while they had been trying to catch Jim to know what they are like. Jim had dismissed it all as my imagination, saying, "Loads of men try to chat you up and, anyway, why would the Dutch police be following us?"

Why indeed.

Howard stayed with us for a few days before heading back home to Oxford.

I liked him and enjoyed his company. He was the exact opposite of Jim; being so laidback he was almost horizontal most of the time. The two of them made an interesting combination, maybe it is true about opposites attracting.

After their first meeting they had quickly gone into business together, a business that was now encroaching on our lives at Kilcoole at an alarming rate. Howard was smuggling drugs and had persuaded Jim that it was an excellent fundraiser for Jim's other interests. If these other interests found out what Jim was doing, he might never live to pass on any profits. I had tried to reason with Jim; he was exchanging ideology for a money-making venture. There was no reasoning with him; as he saw it, money was needed to fund the struggle so he would make as much money as possible and worry about any consequences later.

Howard became a regular visitor to our home and the deals they did expanded into a full-scale business. Jim had set up a dummy business in Dundalk selling office equipment. We had to be able to explain away the amount of traffic coming to the house at all hours of the day and night. He was also now using the outbuildings behind the house as storage.

I managed to escape from the mayhem every now and again. Once to Howard's house in Oxford, which was a complete disaster, more usually to Holland, although now I was so convinced that I was being followed when I went there that I could never really relax.

The lease at Kilcoole was coming to an end. We weren't sure whether to renew it or not; the comings and goings at the house were beginning to attract too much attention from the locals. When I went to the local shop people would be joking about the car conventions we were holding at the house. Once gossip started it would be hard to contain it; we would have to look for somewhere else to live. In the meantime, there were a few jobs we needed to get finished at the house before we handed it back, a major clear-out of the outbuildings being the main one. Another was to sort out the problem with the toilet. It was very slow to flush and there was an unpleasant smell in the garden near the cesspit.

I arranged for the plumbers; Jim organised getting the outbuildings cleared. The cars arrived midweek, they would remove all the packages and deliver them to destinations all over Europe. It would only take a few hours to pack them and get them on their way. Then the plumbers would be here at the end of the week.

Sounded like a plan.

What we had not put into the equation was the propensity for people to not do what they were supposed to do when they said they would do it.

The plumbers arrived early, the drivers arrived late; they all ended up at the house together, there was nothing we could do about it.

As soon as you opened the doors to the outbuildings, the smell of cannabis was overwhelming. The cars were now seriously late so had to be packed and away that day. Jim figured that as long as we kept the plumbers at the house and away from the phone until we knew the cars were safe, it wouldn't be a problem.

The afternoon was rapidly descending into what looked like something out of a carry-on film. Each time the plumbers went to one side of the house the drivers quickly packed a car and moved it then started on the next one; cars were all over the place. It eased up a bit when they had to open up a drain in the front garden. That smell covered up the other to a certain extent. It soon became apparent that we didn't need to worry too much, though. A few hours of walking around the house checking the plumbing whilst inhaling cannabis fumes, and the two plumbers couldn't even remember their own names let alone whether or not they had seen anything unusual.

That week had been too close for comfort. We would have to be more careful in the future.

Apart from all this drama at home, we had also spent a lot of the summer just gone dealing with another of Jim's friends, Conor, who lived in Kerry. It had all started, as it so often did, with a telephone call.

CHAPTER 5

Kerry

Conor was an old friend of Jim's who lived in a beautiful spot in County Kerry on the west coast of Ireland. Jim had told me endless stories of wild times he had spent with Conor; I was never certain how much of these stories were true and how many details had been added for amusement value. But he had assured me that Kerry was beautiful, and he knew that I would love it.

Someone had phoned the house several times at the beginning of that summer and, from what I could make out from the garbled conversation, had wanted to speak to Jim but on each occasion Jim had been out. I had told Jim about the phone calls, saying whoever it was appeared to be drunk, I couldn't really make out what they were trying to tell me, but they appeared to be reciting poetry.

Jim nodded, saying it has to be Conor, he's always drinking, but if he's ringing here, he must be in trouble. "We'll go down at the weekend."

"Oh good, a weekend with an alcoholic." I couldn't wait. Kerry had indeed better be truly spectacular.

Jim reassured me, "It's OK. Callum's parents have a cottage near Conor's house; we can stay there, not at Conor's." Callum was an old friend of Jim's who lived in Dublin.

I had never met Conor but had heard many stories about him from Jim and Callum, who had known him for years. All the stories seemed to involve copious amounts of alcohol. "Kerry is beautiful, you'll love it," Jim assured me again as I tried to come up with more reasons not to go. "We'll have a fantastic weekend."

We set off on Friday afternoon, arriving in the early evening. Jim was right, Kerry was very beautiful. Callum's parents' cottage was picturesque, set back off the road behind a tall hedge on a narrow country lane with a garage to the left side of the house. If you didn't know the cottage was there you could easily miss it. Jim had to concentrate as we drove down the narrow lane to spot the stone pillars set into the hedge that marked the entrance. If you missed the pillars, he said you had to drive over a mile to the local shop before there was enough space to turn the car around.

First job, get the fire going. Although it wasn't particularly cold, nobody had stayed at the cottage for a while, and it needed a bit of heat to take away that sort of damp feeling that places near the sea seem to get if they are not lived in for a while. Fire lit, we headed to Conor's house a mile or so down the lane after the shop. His house was also a cottage with a large sort of lean-to greenhouse at the back. It stood alone overlooking a small bay. The only other building I could see was at the opposite end of the bay.

"That's a convent," Jim said when I asked him what the large building in the distance was, it came into view as we had driven off the road onto a piece of land to the side of Conor's cottage. As the car pulled up, we could hear loud music coming from inside. Somehow, I didn't think there were going to be nuns in there. Conor's cottage was basic to say the least, with not much in the way of furniture: a few random broken dining chairs, a small footstool in the middle of the floor, not much else. The thing that he did have which I loved was a large inglenook fireplace with a cauldron hanging on a large metal bar over the fire. Jim had told me about this. It was permanently cooking a sort of stew. Everything went in the cauldron, from roadkill to rabbits caught in the garden plus bits of vegetables the rabbits didn't manage to get and any leftover dregs of alcohol. There were no mealtimes at Conor's house. Any time you felt hungry you just helped yourself from the cauldron.

The house was packed with an assortment of people of all different ages and descriptions, some singing, some playing various musical instruments with varying degrees of skill. I couldn't make out the song or if in fact they were all playing and singing the same song, the noise in the house was tremendous. Jim saw someone he knew across the room and headed over for a chat. I was left next to what looked like a group of students, three boys and two girls. I introduced myself to them. They told me they were from America on a camping holiday travelling around Ireland before going back to America to start university.

"How do you know Conor?" I asked.

"We don't, we just met him in the pub, and he said we could stay at his house."

How many times had I heard that from Jim? We chatted for a while. I saw Jim across the room having an animated conversation with the person I assumed from Jim's description to be Conor. Jim had an exasperated look on his face, from the look on Conor's face Jim was wasting his time talking to him. He was as Jim had described him – dishevelled, clearly a drinker, and looking years older than he probably was. As the night wore on a few people left, there was a bit more space in the front room now and slowly everyone began to sit in a circle on the floor as space became available. I sat next to one of the American boys and everyone began taking it in turns to do a party-piece. Some people sang, some recited poetry or told jokes. Conor stood on the small stool in the middle of the room and began to recite James Joyce. He had a haunting voice; that and his ability to stand on a small stool whilst drunk had a mesmerising effect on us all. A few hours must have gone by while we had been there, and I suddenly felt really tired although I still wanted to hear the end of Conor's monologue. I looked around for Jim, saw he was still chatting but managed to catch his eye and indicate that I was ready to leave, he gave me the 'in a minute' look, so to try and keep myself awake until Jim was ready to go, I chatted to the boy next to me.

After a while Jim came over and said, "You look tired, let's go."

"Oh, I wanted to hear the end of this." I pointed at Conor. Jim laughed.

"Conor could be there for days. He knows Joyce off by heart and will probably stand on that stool until he has finished the entire book." Jim assured me that we'd come back tomorrow and see if he was sober enough to speak to Jim then. We headed back to Callum's parents' cottage. I hoped the fire was still lit; it was getting cold now.

As we walked into the cottage, an overwhelming feeling of dread engulfed me. I suddenly felt panicky scared of something I couldn't quite understand. I stood looking at the fire, unsure what to say or do. I thought at first it was possibly something I had drunk there had been some strange concoctions on offer at Conor's, but I didn't feel sick at all, just frightened. I debated saying something to Jim but decided against it. I didn't know if I could properly put into words what I was feeling. Maybe if I just concentrated on something else this strange feeling would go away.

Jim said, "If you make the bed, I'll put some more Turf on the fire." In a bit of a dream, I walked upstairs, a huge weight bearing down on my shoulders, my anxiety increasing, every step was a real effort of will to make my legs work. I didn't know what was wrong, I just felt so strange I couldn't shake the feeling of dread, something bad was going to happen. I got a couple of clean sheets from the airing cupboard on the landing and went into the bedroom. Holding two corners, I shook out the sheet ready to throw it across the bed. It was covered in blood. Dropping it with a shriek I ran back downstairs. Jim looked up in surprise as I flung myself at him. He was still kneeling on the floor by the fire. I babbled incoherently. I was saying the right words, they were just not coming out in the right order. He held me until I calmed down a little.

I managed to say, "We have to go, something terrible is going to happen, there is blood everywhere upstairs." Even as I said those words, I knew how strange they must sound; if the blood was everywhere then surely something bad had already happened. I started to grab our things and headed to the front door.

Jim grabbed me and said, "What blood? Where?"

"It's upstairs, all over the sheets."

"If there is blood all over the sheets then something has already happened," Jim said. I was sane, Jim was thinking exactly the same thing as I was; whatever it was, it had already happened. I couldn't argue with that. Calmer now, I said, "Yes it must have already happened. There's nothing we can do about it now. We still have to leave though. I can't spend the night upstairs in this house."

Jim said, "I have to go upstairs and see what's happened, we can't just leave without knowing." I tried my best to try and persuade him not to go upstairs but I did know that he had to look.

All of the sudden, a feeling of dread that had overwhelmed me the second we had entered the cottage had stopped just as abruptly as it had begun, now I just felt completely exhausted, but there was still no way I was going back upstairs.

Jim went up alone and came down a few minutes later, sheets in hand. There were no marks of any sort on either of them.

I looked at the sheets then at Jim and said, "I know what I saw." We talked about it for a while. I had no explanation for what had been happening. One minute I was terrified, scared to death that something awful was going to happen, the next minute I knew it had passed and things would be OK.

Jim told me about the scar on his hand, maybe I had heard about that from Callum and that had frightened me. He and Callum had been down to the cottage some years before and after spending the whole evening drinking had come back to the cottage and not been able to get in. Finding themselves locked out, Jim had broken a small window at the back of the cottage. While he was climbing through the window, he had cut his hand on the broken glass. Callum had then had to cut up an old bedsheet to tie up his hand and stop the bleeding. I listened to Jim, looking for a rational explanation for what had happened to me, but I knew that he had never told me about his hand, neither had Callum, of that much I was certain. Eventually, we took the cushions off the couch and made a makeshift bed and slept downstairs in front of the fire. Nothing Jim said was going to persuade me to go back up those stairs that night, even though I knew the danger, whatever it was, had passed.

*

We woke the following morning and after a leisurely breakfast we headed back to Conor's. Jim wanted to find out what was troubling him. The house had been too busy the previous evening to speak to him properly and Conor had been too drunk to take any notice anyway.

When we arrived at Conor's cottage, the Americans were in the kitchen. We were surprised to see them awake, especially after the amount of drinking that had been going on. They told us they hadn't been to bed yet; they had spent the night in the hospital.

Sarah, one of the girls, said to me, "You remember the boy who was sitting next to you last night?"

"Yes." Couldn't remember his name though.

"Well about half an hour after you and Jim left some of us went outside to set up the tents in Conor's garden. The boy you had been talking to saw the little stream behind the house and went to take a look."

The next thing they heard was a loud splash. He had fallen into the stream. Sarah and the others had to jump in and pull him out. He must have hit his head on a rock because he was unconscious. They had carried him back into Conor's house.

Then Sarah said, "He was bleeding so much we had to wrap his head in a bed sheet. There was blood everywhere, we thought he was going to die."

Someone had run to the pub, the nearest phone, managed to wake the landlord and he had called the ambulance. They were all pretty shaken up by what had happened. It had been several hours before they had been reassured that the boy was ok and with just a few stitches and a couple of days' rest at Conor's he would be fit enough to continue with the trip. He had been so lucky, if nobody had heard him fall in he would almost certainly have drowned.

Jim was quiet throughout the telling of this story. I noticed he was looking at something in the corner of the kitchen. I glanced across, following his gaze to a pile of discarded blood-covered bed sheets on the floor. He looked up at that moment, caught my eye, held my gaze for a moment then looked back at the pile of sheets.

It was impossible to tell from his expression what he was thinking at that moment. I knew what I was thinking, but now was not the time to discuss it. I was just glad that things had turned out OK.

Having heard all of their story, we now needed to speak to Conor and see what was going on with him, that after all had been the reason for our visit in the first place. I was glad that the Americans would be staying a few extra days, it was fun having people of my own age around.

We located Conor and went out into the lean-to with him to have a chat in private.

Things had gotten on top of him. The drinking was out of control, bills were piling up and some stray dogs that he had taken in were now multiplying at an alarming rate. About twenty puppies plus some older dogs were roaming around his garden, some ill, most infested with fleas. Conor couldn't look after himself properly, let alone an army of dogs. He couldn't afford to feed them.

While Jim discussed with him what could be done about the situation, I looked around the lean-to. The entire back wall where it was attached to the house was covered in postcards from all over the world. Not just single postcards spread out but layer upon layer overlapping. There must have been hundreds. I read a few.

They all thanked Conor for allowing them to stay and for the wonderful times they had had at his house.

A plan of action finally agreed upon between Jim and Conor, we went outside to take a look at the puppies. A few were well enough to come back to Kilcoole with us to find new homes. The others were not and ended up having to be put down, as did a lot of the older dogs. They were buried in the back garden. Later that afternoon Jim and I said goodbye to Sarah and the others and headed back to our cottage. We would sleep upstairs tonight.

We stayed an extra few days and then mid-week, with puppies in cardboard boxes on the back seat of the car, we headed back to Kilcoole. All things considered I had enjoyed our time in Kerry.

Some months later we headed back to Kerry to see how Jim's plan of action was working out.

We hadn't had any phone calls from Conor so hoped that meant things were going well. Jim and I would stay at Callum's parents' cottage again. Jim had spoken to Callum about our strange experience the last time we had stayed there.

Callum was a trainee doctor, so, according to Jim, he of course would know exactly what had happened.

There was no logical explanation, I knew that, so refused to discuss it with Callum. I also knew it had really freaked Jim out, he needed a logical explanation, not me, I was just happy to accept it for what it was.

Callum came up with the theory that years ago when Jim had cut his hand at the cottage and Callum had bandaged it, one of them must have told me about it at some point. Jim still had the scar; I must have asked him about that. Jim must have told me all about it and the rest was just coincidence. I didn't bother to point out the obvious flaws in that theory, the main one being that none of us could ever remember discussing how Jim had got the scar on his hand.

I just hoped that Callum wouldn't decide to go into psychiatry.

We arrived at the cottage late in the evening and decided to get a night's sleep before going to Conor's. The following morning, I checked the kitchen: no supplies. Jim would have to go to the shop if we wanted any breakfast. He was still half asleep but moaning that he was hungry.

"You're going to have to get up and get dressed if you want any breakfast. There's no food in the house," I said.

"It's about time you learnt to drive," he said.

"Good idea." I could take some lessons when we got back to Kilcoole.

Jim said, "The shop's only a mile away. You've seen me drive often enough," and he gave me the car keys.

OK, how difficult could this be?

I got dressed and headed to the car.

The route to the shop was a narrow lane, only a single car wide with passing places. The chances of other vehicles on the road would be minimal. I should be able to get there and back, although turning around at the shop might be a bit tricky.

Luckily the car was facing out onto the road. I started it all right but stalled a few times before I managed to figure out how to get it moving in first gear. I managed to get the car out of the gateway and onto the road without any mishap, things were going really well, I was doing fine but couldn't quite manage to get the car into any other gear. Each time I tried it made a horrendous noise, so I thought, *at least it's moving, and I'll just drive there in first gear.*

As I approached the shop, it occurred to me that I wasn't entirely certain how you stopped a car. Was it enough to just put your foot on the brake or did you have to do anything else? Too late to worry about that now, I turned the wheel too fast, braked too late, and crashed into the small wall in front of the shop.

Luckily that small wall was there otherwise I would have been doing the shopping without needing to get out of the car.

The car had stalled. I remembered about the handbrake, put that on, then checked the damage to the car and the wall. Thankfully not too bad. Jim was going to be a bit annoyed about this, but he had given me the keys, so he was at least partly to blame.

Still, I was here now so might as well get the groceries. I just hoped the car would start again. It was a long walk back to the house with all the shopping I needed to get if it didn't. Shopping done, apologies given, plus details of how the shop could get payment for the repairs needed to the wall, I headed back to the car for the homeward journey.

Back in the car, I tried starting it again.

It went first time. I was getting good at this. I tried to get into reverse; got that, so far so good. Just go backwards now, that should be it. I went backwards slowly. I was getting the hang of this now, but the lane was so narrow I would need to do a three-point turn to get the car facing the way I needed to go. I very nearly managed it before the back of the car hit that small wall again and it stalled again. Oh well, they had all my details, I didn't need to give the shop owner my details again. My initial confidence was ebbing away now, and I still had to get back to the cottage. At least the car was more-or-less facing in the right direction. I got into first gear and set off slowly back to the cottage. On the way back I suddenly panicked, thinking about how I was going to get the car back through the concrete gate posts at the cottage. If I missed the entrance I would have to drive for miles before I could turn around. I couldn't face trying to reverse again, maybe I could just stop the car in the lane and Jim could drive it in. Caught up in all these thoughts, I didn't realize how far I had already driven. At the last minute I spotted the stone pillars, panicking I swung the car left into the driveway much too hard. The car hit the pillar and scraped all down the left-hand side of the vehicle. Now in even more of a panic, listening to the horrific screaming of concrete against metal, I turned the wheel in the opposite direction as hard as I could. The rear of the car swung wildly, hitting the other pillar with an almighty crash and the car then bounced into the dustbins at the side of the garage and came to a stop. My head bounced into the windscreen, and I too came to a stop and sat there dazed.

Jim had heard the commotion and when I went into the cottage a few moments later, he asked me if I had done any damage hitting the bins.

"No, not really. I did the damage hitting the shop and then the pillars."

"What?" He went outside. A few minutes later I heard him kicking the bins. I left him for a while and then when I thought the bins had had enough punishment for one day, I followed him outside.

"How the hell did you do so much damage?"

I told him what had happened. He was still fuming so I had to say, "Please stop shouting. I have a really bad headache." Then, "I thought you loved me."

He did love me, I knew that, but as he told me more than once that day, he was pretty fond of his car as well.

Several days later we finally made it to Conor's house, the delay caused by the lack of being able to communicate with anyone. The nearest phone was at the shop. Jim had surveyed the damaged shop wall when we got there and had agreed a price to cover the damage then we had used their phone to ring a mechanic then back to the cottage to wait for him to arrive.

The news had not been good. The car was a write-off.

The following day it had been another trek to the shop to organise another car then back to the cottage to wait for it to arrive.

At least we had some groceries to keep us from starving.

No wonder life was so slow around here. At least the people in the shop were still friendly and on my side. Jim had paid for the damage to their wall, and they had agreed with me when I said it was all his fault really. He had given me the keys.

It was a surprise to find Sarah still at Conor's house when we finally got back there. The other Americans had gone home months ago.

It soon became obvious that she was in a relationship with Conor, although she hadn't said a word when we'd arrived. The usually bubbly chatty girl was totally silent. She sat with what could only be described as a serene smile on her face and only nodded or shook her head to yes or no questions. Jim was exasperated and said to me, "Why don't you two go for a swim while I talk to Conor."

Sarah and I headed to the beach. Maybe she would speak to me if we were alone together.

A little superfluity of nuns was on the water's edge at the opposite end of the beach. Some were removing their shoes, others already paddling. They looked like a little flock of black and white birds fluttering at the water's edge. Delicately, they lifted their long skirts. Wouldn't do to expose their ankles, even on this virtually deserted beach. Next to me Sarah was silently undressing. Distracted by the nun's I didn't notice until it was too late that she had removed all of her clothes, then, with a whoop, which at least proved she hadn't been struck dumb by something, she ran naked across the long stretch of beach and into the sea. Startled by the sudden noise and the sight of a naked, obviously pregnant girl running down the beach, the little black and white birds had panicked and then scattered back to the convent, skirts flying.

I joined Sarah in the water, and we had a long swim. I was putting off the moment we would have to go back to the house and tell Jim this latest, now-only-too-apparent bit of news. I tried talking to her about the baby: had she seen a doctor, what was she going to do when it arrived? No answers to anything. I wasn't even sure if she understood that she was pregnant.

Back at the house Jim wasn't getting on much better. At least Conor understood that Sarah was pregnant but had done nothing about it.

When the other Americans had left to continue their

holiday, Sarah had decided to stay behind with Conor.

After their first night together, Sarah had stopped talking to anyone, including him. She just sat and smiled her serene smile and nodded or shook her head.

We couldn't leave the situation as it was. Sarah was only a young girl, Conor old enough to be her father. That evening we looked through her belongings. We told her beforehand what we were doing and why. She just smiled and nodded. It was very unnerving.

Having found an ID in her belongings, we told them both that we were going to contact Sarah's parents when we got back to Kilcoole to see what they wanted us to do. Jim and I were at a loss to know how to handle this situation, but something had to be done, and soon, she would need help when the baby was born if nothing else.

The conversation with Sarah's mother was tough, so hard to try and explain something we really didn't understand ourselves.

In the end, a few weeks later, Sarah's mother flew to Ireland and came to stay at our house at Kilcoole, having refused to go to Kerry or have anything to do with Conor.

In the week before she arrived, we went down to Kerry and told Sarah that her mother was coming to our house at Kilcoole the following week. Sarah smiled, went upstairs, got her things, and without a backward glance at Conor, got into the back seat of our car. We drove home to Kilcoole that evening and settled her in our spare room to wait for her mother's arrival. Even with her mother in front of her, Sarah still didn't speak, just smiled.

Her mother booked tickets for them both to go home to America. When asked if she wanted to go home with her mother, Sarah had smiled and nodded her head.

We drove them both to the airport. As we hugged them goodbye and said we hoped everything would be OK, Sarah turned to me and said, "Thank you."

Then she smiled her beautiful, serene smile and was gone. Whatever strange spell had bewitched her in Kerry seemed to be lifting.

Having experienced something so strange myself when I had been in Kerry, I was just happy to accept it for what it was and hope that when she got home, she would be ok.

We heard from Sarah's mother a few times after that but never from Sarah herself, although she was talking again and appeared to be completely back to her former self.

The baby was born safely, and the decision was made that it would be better for all concerned if Sarah and the baby remained in America. We had found homes for all the puppies by then too.

Now, with the lease about to run out at Kilcoole, we just needed to find a new home for us too.

CHAPTER 6

Belfast

After news of our engagement was out, Jim's family began to have a different attitude to our relationship. I didn't blame them for their initial response. Jim was the eldest and had brought home a girlfriend fourteen years younger than himself and a British one at that.

When we had first met and then started seeing each other, I wasn't even old enough to buy a drink or vote. Still a child really, no matter how grown up I had felt at the time.

Our initial separation had probably given them hope that I was only a passing fad but then the effort that Jim had made to get me back must have left them in no doubt that he was serious about me and now we were officially engaged.

I was going to Belfast to meet Jim's sister, who I hadn't yet met, and spend some time with her and her family. I had a photograph of her. She would meet me at Belfast railway station. Should be no problem. My fake passport had been fine on all the flights we had taken so just had to show it when asked at the border and not say too much if at all possible. Hopefully the soldiers at the border wouldn't ask me any questions. My passport stated that I was Irish but, try as I might, I couldn't manage a decent fake Irish accent. It always sounded as though I was trying to make fun of it. I showed my passport at the border when asked and said nothing. The border patrol thankfully asked no questions and the train continued on into Belfast.

As it travelled into the city whose very name was synonymous with trouble, I looked out at scenes I had only seen on TV news programmes. Very strange feeling to be travelling through the middle of it now.

The rules I needed to remember kept replaying in my mind. Jim had gone over them so many times, not trying to frighten me, just to try and make me aware exactly how dangerous a position I would be in. I was going to be entering a war zone and needed to keep my wits about me. Only certain religions used taxis, others used buses. Would I remember which ones the Catholics used? If I got it wrong, I could be dead before anyone even realised I was missing. It was what they might do to me before they killed me that played on my mind the most.

The train was slowing down, then pulled abruptly to a stop. I could see a large crowd of armed soldiers on the platform, far more than I had expected would be here, maybe they were waiting to catch a train. Just needed to act casual, I kept telling myself, look as though I did this all the time and make my way to the front of the station to wait for Mary.

As my foot touched the platform, a loud bang filled the station and the whole place began to shake. The initial bang was not that great but the reverberations that succeeded it were deafening. It was hard to keep my footing. My ears felt as though they were going to explode at any moment, then a second of silence, immediately followed by a massive sucking in of air. I had gone deaf. It felt as though all the oxygen was being sucked out of the place. I couldn't breathe and struggled hard to contain the panic that was engulfing me. I could taste acid in my mouth and thought I would vomit then or pass out. Earthquake had been the first thought that entered my head, then gradually the realisation filtered in: you're in Belfast, it must have been a bomb.

Strange how we have fixed ideas about how things will be until we actually experience them, and the reality is so different from what we had expected or imagined. Apart from a few things out of place around the station, everything else looked pretty normal and as you would expect it to be. As I put my second foot on the platform, still trying desperately to get the panic under control, I could sense my hearing slowly going back to normal, the ringing in my ears was subsiding and panic was abating a little. I risked a look around; the roof and walls were still in place so whatever it was hadn't actually happened in the railway station. Must have been somewhere close by though, the rest of the train seemed to be intact as well, the bomb, if that was really what the noise had been, must have exploded outside the station. There were clouds of dust in the air, you could see and smell it. The other passengers behind me were getting off the train now. The people who had been on the platform and had instinctively ducked for shelter were now standing back up again, dusting themselves down, picking up dropped bags, and then quietly heading for the exit. The whole scene was so quiet, so peaceful, it was eerie in its serenity. No-one screaming, running about hysterically crying, just people getting back to their day, almost as though absolutely nothing out of the ordinary had occurred. Maybe for them it hadn't. The soldiers for their part were doing exactly the same thing. I stood a moment, gathering my thoughts after what had just happened. What if Mary failed to turn up, what should I do then?

I composed myself as well as I could, initial panic having subsided a little more, then followed the crowd calmly out of the station to wait outside for my prospective new sister-in-law. I found a bench outside the station and sat down to read my book and try not to attract attention. What I was not to know, thankfully, was that the bomb had been in a hotel close to the railway station and there was every possibility that the bombers may have planted a second device. All traffic into and out of the area had been stopped and an initial perimeter set up, anyone trying to get into the immediate area was facing detailed questioning. The first hour passed by. In all the advice that Jim had given me before I left home, he had never imagined the possibility that Mary might not arrive at the station.

Another hour passed, now I was seriously worried, the trains seemed to be running again, maybe I should just go back to Dublin. I had no way of contacting Mary though. I decided to give it one more hour and if she hadn't arrived by then I would get on the next train and go back to Dublin.

Thankfully, half an hour later she made it to the station. I was so relieved. So was she, having not fancied having to make a phone call to Jim saying I was lost somewhere in Belfast. She told me about the roadblocks and the questioning, I told her about my feelings once I realized it was a bomb and how close it had been to the railway station. My initial fright had given way to anger at the thought of what could have happened. How did people live like this, surrounded by fear every day just going about their day-to-day activities? I was relieved to be in Mary's car and heading away from the station.

Mary's home was on the outskirts of Belfast. It was very clean and tidy, and I immediately felt at home, Mary was so welcoming. We telephoned Jim to let him know we were both ok. It was a strange conversation, whilst I had been sitting reading for a few hours once the initial shock had worn off, Jim had been at home worrying. It hadn't occurred to me to think about how Jim would be feeling and what he would be thinking or that he would even know about it.

I knew I was ok. He didn't. Having seen the news programmes he had then had to wait over three hours before he knew that I was unhurt, also that Mary had not been caught in the blast outside while on the way to collect me. I kept thinking that maybe delayed shock would set in but somehow my mind just sort of accepted what had happened and was calm about the whole thing.

Maybe it would have been different if there had been injured people and I had seen them, I hoped I wouldn't ever have to find out. I spent the next few weeks with Mary and her family, just doing normal family things, or at least trying to.

It was good to walk a mile in her shoes, see what life was like for them in what was essentially a war zone or at the very least an occupied country.

I was trying to understand what Jim's life had been like as a child growing up in this environment of hatred and mistrust and what influences had persuaded him to take the path he was currently on. I could leave this place whenever I wanted to, Mary and her family were stuck here for the duration, however long that might be.

The big restrictions you got used to very quickly, it was the small things that got to me the most. I had to avoid speaking when other people could hear me, if at all possible, my accent would have given me away immediately and that would have put not only me but Mary and her family in danger. I went into Belfast with Mary on one of her usual shopping trips, she had told me we would be walking some of the way and would have to go through several checkpoints manned by British soldiers. Definitely had to keep my mouth shut for that bit.

The fact that security at the shops was so tight seemed like a good thing to me, we would be relatively safe, surely. Since my experience at the railway station, we had only gone out in the car and I was a bit nervous at the thought of being on foot. Mary reassured me then and said, "At the checkpoint, say nothing, just wait for them to finish searching you then walk on."

"Ok no problem," I said. How wrong could I have been? When Mary said they would search us, I assumed she meant they would look in my bag, check my pockets, give a quick pat down maybe and that would be it. We joined the queue at the first checkpoint and waited our turn. Mary went through first. When it was my turn I moved forward cautiously to a soldier, a complete stranger to me, who was also carrying a gun, who in seconds had touched my breasts and squeezed them and had then moved both hands down between my legs, one rubbing the front of my body, the other my bottom. He looked me directly in the eyes, daring me to do something while he carried on rubbing my body and making lewd comments to his colleague. I stood frozen to the spot, so angry I had to fight the urge to punch him in the face. How could this be happening in a public place and perpetrated by the very people who were supposed to be keeping everyone safe? If I had been in England, I would have accused these men of sexual assault. Here, the women just had to put up with it, hard to argue with men who have guns. We had to go through several of these checkpoints, both going into the city centre and leaving that day. Some were run properly and were no problem, the ones that weren't were a real ordeal for me and I seriously struggled with my anger about this the whole day. As we went through each one, Mary went first and once she was through she turned to face me, and I concentrated on looking at her and ignoring what they were doing. It helped.

It spoilt what should have been a relaxing day for Mary though and I was sorry about that.

But it was good that I had experienced it first-hand so to speak. I did struggle sometimes to understand where Jim's anger came from every time he spoke about Belfast and what was happening in his country.

I was at boiling point after just one day of this treatment, he had endured things like this the whole time he was growing up. No wonder he chose to fight back, as did so many others.

On the way back to Mary's house one afternoon we had to pass one of the main army barracks. We had driven past it several times previously. There was a large grassed mounded roundabout like a small hill in front of the heavily fortified building which, because of its size and height, loomed over this whole area like a massive dark cloud. As the car slowed for the roundabout, I was aware of a strange noise, it seemed to be coming from the roundabout itself. I couldn't make out exactly what the noise was. Then I heard the sound of metal on metal banging and crashing. What the hell was going on? The closer we got to the roundabout, the louder the noise was becoming. I couldn't hear what Mary was saying to me but, judging by the fact that we were slowing down and not speeding up to get away from it, I figured she must know what it was. As we drove around the roundabout people on the far side that we hadn't previously been able to see came into view.

Each of them had an assortment of objects, bin lids, saucepans, large ladles tools of all descriptions, anything metal, and they were banging them with sticks, spoons, old bits of wood, whatever seemed to have come to hand to make the worst noise imaginable. It had to be some sort of protest.

The shocking thing for me was the numbers of children in the group, some of them only seemed to be about five or six and to be in the middle of that din surely must have been very frightening for them. I looked up at the towers on the barracks, armed soldiers were in the towers which were placed at intervals all along the walls, it was very intimidating. It was after several minutes more of driving before I could hear Mary again. She explained that someone must have been arrested and was probably being held at the barracks for questioning and that was what they were protesting about.

Internment without trial had been brought in during the summer; people could be held in prison indefinitely without being convicted of any crime and with precious little in the way of legal advice or help. It was so unjust that every time they arrested someone a protest took place. It all seemed so surreal to me. How could you put someone in prison and not give them a trial? Mary just smiled at my obvious confusion about how this could happen. Clearly, I still had a lot to learn about life in Belfast.

"How long will the protest go on?" I asked her.

"Probably all night," she said. "At some point they will attack the barracks." We sat in Mary's house and listened to the continuing noise that was getting louder, more people must have gathered and be joining in the protest.

As it began to go dark outside, the mixture of noises melted into one sound like a drumbeat with an exact rhythm – thump thump thump – all the other noises joined it and the sounds of the people who had been shouting gradually died away.

I sat in the house listening to the changing sounds and remembering the sight of the fortified barracks looming over the roundabout. It reminded me of all the cowboy films I had watched growing up where the Indians sit around the campfire drumming slowly and then getting faster and faster until they attack the fort.,

But what could they hope to achieve, I asked they couldn't get into the barracks?

"No, they can't," said Mary, "but whoever is inside can hear them and know that they haven't been forgotten. People are still doing their best and trying to get them out."

The beat was slowly, oh so slowly, increasing.

Although we were some distance away from the roundabout and barracks, the effects on us, I imagined, were the same as on those who were closer. It became impossible to do anything else other than listen. The beat got into your head and then slowly into the rest of your body, the tension increasing with the increasing beat, it felt as though my head would explode. Then, with my heart beating out of my chest, I waited for it to be over.

Finally, around midnight the beat was so fast I was nearly hyper ventilating, then, with a huge noise of shouting and jeering, the attack had obviously begun. Mainly they would throw rocks or whatever else they could get their hands on at the huge, fortified walls Mary told me, that would go on until they ran out of rocks or until the soldiers in the guard towers began to shoot at them. "But there are children there." I always felt foolish when I said things like that, the expression on Mary's face as I said it was almost pitying. I really didn't understand what things were like here, even though I had experienced some of it. The rules that I had been taught all my life simply didn't apply here anymore. Visit over, it was time to get back to Jim.

*

I flew to Holland to meet up with Jim who had gone to stay with some old friends Lucas and Sophie while I was in Belfast. They lived in a small town in the south of Holland. I couldn't wait to see him again. I had enjoyed staying with his sister and meeting some of his other relatives, but Belfast was a strain for me and for them. The responsibility of having to keep me safe must have been a real worry for them. It was time we all had a rest. I was pleased I would be staying with Jim's friends. I always enjoyed their company and was looking forward to a relaxing few weeks.

CHAPTER 7

Kenya

Africa? You're joking? When? For how long? I was so excited I could barely speak, well apart from the twenty questions I had already bombarded Jim with. He was laughing at my excitement, trying to answer the torrent of questions raining down on him. Yes, we were going in a few weeks to Kenya. We were going to fly from Frankfurt to Nairobi and then take an overnight train to Mombasa, arriving just in time to see the sun coming up.

The last summer in Kilcoole and the mess up over the departure, plus all of the Conor stuff, had been hectic, as had my stay in Belfast. Jim and I both needed some time alone together.

The next few weeks flew by, marred only by the thought of all the injections that would be needed before we went. I am absolutely terrified of needles. Every attempt by Jim to persuade me to get them done had failed miserably. He had tried everything, from gentle coaxing to trying to embarrass me about it and eventually threats that he would go on his own and leave me behind. There was not a lot left for him to try, or so I thought. It wasn't as though I didn't want to go. Quite the opposite, it's just that a phobia is so totally irrational it is really hard to explain that fear to someone who doesn't have that fear, and time was running out. Couldn't we get fake injection certificates? I had pleaded with him. Yes, we could of course but he wouldn't do it. The illnesses that you could pick up in Africa were too severe, they could kill me. He refused to take that risk.

A phone call interrupted one pleading session. "If you loved me, you wouldn't make me have them," I had said, close to tears.

Counter argument from Jim: "It's because I love you that I won't take you without having the inoculations." I'd try sulking next, see how that worked. The look on Jim's face was serious as he listened to whoever was on the other end of the phone call and then he said, "Which hospital?" That stopped me in my attempt at a sulk. It would never have worked anyway. Jim always made me laugh.

He listened for a few more moments then said, "OK, see you there in half an hour."

"What's wrong?" I asked.

"That was Lucas, Sophie's in hospital. They don't know what's wrong, but it looks serious." We grabbed our coats and headed for the car. We had only seen them a few hours earlier and she had seemed fine. Jim said, "don't worry, Lucas is with her." I had such a sick feeling in my stomach I thought I was going to vomit. Jim kept trying to reassure me.

The journey, although only about twenty minutes, seemed like an eternity.

At last, we pulled into what looked like a large office block and parked. It is one of the strange things about being in other countries when you can't speak or read the language. Buildings that you would recognise at home become unfamiliar and a written sign does not always tell you what you need to know, no matter how big it is. They should have pictures instead. We went up in the lift and then along a corridor. We could see Lucas waiting at the end.

"She's in here," he said, pointing to a door with a name plaque on and some letters and writing underneath. He and Jim ushered me into the room. It was only as the door closed behind me that I realised they had each taken hold of one of my arms. Still trying to ask Lucas how Sophie was and confused about why they had a hold of my elbows, I looked around to see where she was.

In front of us was not Sophie as I had expected but a man behind a desk. What the heck was happening? Before I had time to react, Lucas and Jim propelled me to a chair in front of the desk and pushed me down into it. Jim quickly moved behind the chair and pinned me down. At the same time Lucas had made a grab for my legs and ended up having to sit on my feet to keep me down. He was a lot smaller than Jim and having sat on my feet he still needed to grab me around the knees to keep me still.

I tried hard to struggle, especially when I saw the

injections heading in my direction, but I was going nowhere fast with the two of them holding me down. Exhausted with the effort to shake off the two of them, I gave in and stopped struggling. Only crying left. The doctor finished what he had to do and wrote out what Jim told me later was my injection certificate.

Lucas and Jim released my arms at last and we were free to leave. As we walked back down the corridor to the lift, such a tumult of emotion was rushing through me that I didn't know which one to deal with first. Anger welled up foremost, not because they had held me down but because of the half hour I had spent worrying about Sophie, then the relief of knowing that she was OK. Then anger again because they had held me down, then relief because they had held me down and the dreaded injections had been done, then anger again – this could go on all day.

We had reached the lift. I was still crying. Jim had watched the changing emotions the length of the corridor, waiting to see which reaction would explode in his direction first.

They stood behind me as the lift doors closed. I turned around and glared at each of them in turn then squeezed between them. If they honestly thought that I would trust either of them to stand behind me again they had to be joking. The ride to the ground was made in silence. As the doors opened, I stepped out first, looked at a lovely sunny but cold winter's day in Holland and thought in a few weeks we would be in Africa. Thanks guys, it needed to be done. I turned and hugged them both. That didn't mean they were totally off the hook though, Lucas could be spared as he was only doing what Jim wanted, but Jim would definitely get some retribution at some point, just not today. I was in relief mode again. I would have to wait for anger mode then sort him out.

We stayed overnight in Frankfurt to be at the airport in time for the flight that morning. As the plane taxied towards the terminal building, I looked in awe at the size of the thing. I had seen Jumbo jets at airports before but always from a distance. I had not realized how big they were. We were sitting in the first-floor lounge of the terminal building as the plane taxied towards us. The plane's windows were above our heads and there were two rows of windows. They had an upstairs. How did something this size ever get off the ground? Even Jim was getting excited now. Being older than me, he had developed the 'adult' air and always tried to have the been-there-done-that attitude to the outside world. I didn't care what people thought, I was excited and quite happy for everyone to know it. The take-off was a worrying affair this time, being now used to the usual time it took for a plane to leave the ground, this time it didn't happen. Instead, we lumbered on for what seemed like an age. I resisted the urge to shout out "We're going to run out of runway!" It might have started a panic, opting instead to grip Jim's hand ever tighter. At last, with one almighty effort, the front end lifted off the ground and we were leaning back in our seats, looking at the ceiling that still left the back of the plane on the ground, struggling to get airborne.

It reminded me of how my grandfather used to get out of an armchair: he used to press his hands on the arms of the armchair, then with an almighty effort raise his butt out of the seat, stand for a moment to get his balance, then walk. The arms bit seemed to have gone OK. We were stalled on the butt-out-of-the-seat bit. I looked around. Was there any spare weight we could lose, odd bits of luggage, occasional passengers nobody would miss? I started making a mental list. The front was already off the ground, maybe we could all move forward slowly until we seesawed the back off the ground. Odd the thoughts that come into your head when sitting strapped into a seat with nothing to do and no real way of changing what is happening. I did not like this lack of control; it reminded me too much of injection day. After what seemed like an eternity, the plane was fully off the ground, and we were levelling off in the air now. We just had to sit here for the best part of a day until we got to Nairobi.

Time to play with the freebies: slippers, pillow, blanket, disposable toothbrush – the list went on. Lunch was served. Always a surprise how many different bits of disposable plastic could contain various food items, none of which ever tasted like what they looked like. The disposable cutlery was so flimsy you could never pick up anything with the fork or cut anything with the knife, the only useful thing being the spoon as long as you didn't bite it. The flight was longer than any I had been on before and began to get really boring after about six hours. Jim was bored too and started one of his favourite games of seeing where we could spend some time alone together. Not always easy but usually do-able, even if only very quickly. The answer is, yes, you can. The answer to the follow-up question is, no, I'm not going to say where or how. Have fun finding out for yourself. If I told everyone they might have to re-design the plane to stop it rocking in flight.

After what seemed like an eternity, we were at last descending into Nairobi airport. Most of the passengers had slept for the last couple of hours and were now awoken with hot lemon-scented towels to freshen up with. The descent was slow and ponderous. If I had been worried about the take-off, the thought of this gigantic chunk of metal belly flopping onto the ground now occupied my thoughts even more. Chuck some people overboard, did you still call it overboard when it is a plane not a boat? Such an obvious solution, why didn't they just open the door and start jettisoning some of them now? I was sure they would still stand a chance if they gave them parachutes. They would be hailed as heroes, jumping to save the rest of us. Might not get enough volunteers, though. Might have to push a few just to be sure we had lost enough weight. It certainly took my mind off what was happening to think crazy thoughts. My musings were interrupted by the plane thumping onto the ground. So far so good. We were down; still going at an incredible speed though, and then the brakes kicked in. The G force welded me to the back of the seat as the brakes screeched and screeched to stop the plane before we ran out of runway. Finally, we definitely stopped, and I tried to get out of my seat, arms first, then slowly, oh so slowly, my butt. Sitting for so long, I had turned into my grandfather. My whole body seemed to have seized up. Now I knew why the plane had struggled so much.

We spent a few nights in Nairobi acclimatising to the heat before taking the overnight train to Mombasa and the coast. I always preferred to be near the sea now if at all possible. The train was old and slow, trundling majestically across the African landscape. It must have once been a beautiful thing but was now well past its best. The marble sink in the corner of the compartment with its large mahogany lid was still beautiful, as was the carved woodwork, but all the upholstery was shabby, as were the window coverings. The bunk beds had gleaming white starched sheets and the whole compartment was spotlessly clean. We had our own attendant to look after us while we travelled, dressed in a spotless starched uniform. He summoned us to the dining car for the evening meal and then served us a delicious meal of freshly prepared fish and meat. It was like something out of an Agatha Christie novel. The only thing missing was the corpse.

We went back to our compartment after dinner and settled down for an early night. We wanted to be up to see the African landscape and maybe some animals at sunrise before it all got swallowed up by the urban sprawl of Mombasa. As light began to come into the compartment, I was aware of Jim standing by the sink, having a strip wash. He had just got to an interesting bit, and I watched him lazily, opening my eyes now and again, still trying to decide whether I was awake or not. A sudden thought came into my head. If he wanted to brush his teeth, he would need to use bottled water.

I said, "Don't forget that's not drinking water." I had startled him. He hadn't realised that I was awake. He jumped and turned slightly towards me. I seemed to have startled the train as well because it gave a sharp jolt and shudder before regaining its usual momentum. At that same moment, with a loud crash that echoed around the compartment, the heavy mahogany lid hit the unsuspecting sink, missing by a hair's breadth the equally unsuspecting Jim, who just managed to remove a part of himself that he held quite dear before it got mangled to a pulp. Face white even through his suntan, he looked down to check it really was all still there. My face in contrast was bright red. I was choking with laughter, tears running down my face. For a good few minutes Jim failed to see the funny side of what had just happened. Shock evaporating, he eventually started to see the funny side and, laughing, jumped on me, holding my arms down. I couldn't struggle, I was still convulsing with laughter. He said, "Now I'm just going to have to spend some time checking it all still works OK." By the time he had re-assured himself that all was still functioning OK, we were only about an hour away from Mombasa.

We watched the world go by for the rest of the journey. Small groups of thatched mud huts dotted the view, naked men walking about outside, stretching, having just woken up and children playing in the dust. I wondered how they survived without running water, electricity, shops and all the other things that we are so used to and so readily take for granted. It seemed so odd to be viewing people like this, almost as though we were nosing in through their windows, although we in fact were the ones inside looking out. I wondered what they thought about us. Were they as curious about how we lived as we were about them and their lives?

The train was beginning to pass through what looked like a large rubbish tip, the mounds of rubbish about ten feet high but getting taller and closer together the further we went. The first few flies were on the windows and increasing rapidly. By the time the rubbish mounds were taller than the train, the view was obliterated by millions of flies and bluebottles all trying to catch a free ride on this potential new moving feast. We ate breakfast in the dining car with all the lights on. Very little daylight was getting in now and it was hard to have any sort of an appetite. Even though the food looked really good again, there were so many millions of eyes watching from only inches away and noisily buzzing, waiting for any potential leftovers, that I couldn't eat. Gradually we were moving clear of the rubbish. The flies were beginning to clear too, opting to stay where they knew there was definitely a free meal to be had. The view returned and now we were in the urban sprawl, and a short time later the railway station.

A friend of Jim's, who had an interest in a hotel on the beach in Mombasa, met us at the station and took us to the hotel. It was stunningly beautiful: little chalets dotted under palm trees in well-kept gardens, each with a small enclosed private area. The main building housed a restaurant and bar with flats above. We would be in one of the flats until a chalet became available. The beach itself had beautiful white sand sloping gently to the azure ocean that stretched as far as the eye could see. The sky was a brilliant dazzling shade of blue with only a few wispy white clouds dotted here and there. It was nearly impossible to go outside without sunglasses, the light was so brilliant, the heat making everything shimmer. The only drawback marring this picture of perfection was that, because of frequent muggings, tourists and lone women in particular were advised not to walk on the beach by themselves but to stay in the hotel grounds, especially at night.

Whereas the George V in Paris had been magnificent for its opulent interiors, this hotel by contrast was magnificent for having nothing much exceptional at all except its view, and that was more than enough to rival anywhere else we had been. We settled into our rooms and spent the day lazing on the loungers in the shade, still acclimatising to the heat and planning what we wanted to do while we were here. Later we dressed and went for dinner in the restaurant. The food was excellent local fish cooked simply; absolutely delicious. The company was good, too. A group of tourists from the hotel were in the bar and, as is his way, Jim was soon buying everyone drinks and regaling them with stories. Only the facts were altered just to make the stories more interesting, otherwise they were completely true, although different at every telling. If Jim was around and there was any sort of an audience, willing or unwilling, it was always party time as far as he was concerned. It was hard to keep up with him at times. I had partied hard at college but living with Jim was something different altogether. At college we had always had to limit the fun during the week due to the necessity to get up the following morning and actually do some work. Now with Jim there were no restrictions and parties could go on for days, tiredness and the need to sleep the only things usually stopping the fun. I lost track of how long this one lasted but was vaguely aware of staff changes at the bar happening fairly regularly. Other than that, the party continued, and they kept the bar open.

Slowly the tourists drifted away to their rooms and, with only a few stragglers left, Jim and I headed back to our room, too. I have a vague recollection of undressing a little trail of clothes, marking my track across the bedroom and collapsing in a heap onto the bed and then oblivion.

Waking after a party is never as much fun as you would think it might be, happy party memories flooding back to relive again, half-remembered jokes to laugh at anew, any silliness performed by one of the drunken tourists to remember. Instead, the only thing that's liable to come flooding back is whatever you had for your last meal and that maybe more than once, thanks for the memories that just kept on giving. This particular post-party day had left me with a thumping headache and taste memories of what I thought a mouthful of Mombasa's rubbish tip might be like. There was also an extremely strange feeling going on between my legs. Hard to describe exactly, something between an annoying itch and a burning heat sensation. Opening my eyes, a fraction, I surveyed our bedroom, conscious that Jim was asleep beside me, snoring quietly. I tried to look around without disturbing him. My eyes slowly focused and I lifted my head off the pillow. Bad mistake. I momentarily focused on the trail of discarded clothes before dropping my head back onto the pillow as gently as possible. Even that hurt though. Would have to be a bit less ambitious, maybe just start with getting my eyes properly open before trying anything as ambitious as moving.

After a short break to gather some strength, I tried the eye opening again. I had died and gone to heaven: there was a large fluffy white angel hovering over me. *Pull yourself together* flashed through my mind. I didn't believe in all that. Realisation dwindled in through the headache. What was it everyone had said about making sure that we put the mosquito net down every night? Couldn't be that vital, surely.

Though they had seemed to think that it was pretty important when they told us last night. We would have to remember from now on. Too late to worry about that for now, though. The urge to go to the toilet was overwhelming even the headache. I ran to the bathroom, figuring a short sharp burst of headache pain was better than a slow walk. I was quickly sorry that I had gotten there so fast; the urine washed over something down below so painful I let out a scream. I heard Jim stir, no mad rush to save me though, obviously he had a similar headache. I slowly hobbled back into the bedroom.

Jim was more awake now and listened while I told him something was definitely not right. After some discussion the conclusion was that I must have been bitten by a mosquito. Nasty but not that serious. We had some cream that should sort it out. We showered, dressed, and went to the restaurant for some food, both hungry now. I couldn't remember how long it had been since we last ate anything. Heads still a little fuzzy but getting better. We were the first of the group to appear that day. As we ate the others began to appear in dribs and drabs. I had to endure endless amounts of teasing about my current problem, it was impossible to hide the fact that something was wrong. It even hurt to sit down, and I was now actively avoiding having to go to the loo. By late evening the pain was really bad so I went to bed early, hoping it would ease by morning.

No such luck. When I awoke next morning, the pain was even worse, and it felt as though I had a football jammed between my thighs. This couldn't be just a mozzie bite, surely.

By late afternoon, going to the toilet was impossible, I was just too swollen. Jim took a look then spoke to his friends. We needed to see a doctor and sooner rather than later; they would arrange it for us. Within an hour they were driving us on our way to the doctor's house; he would see me straight away. We arrived at a small house on the outskirts of Mombasa. The doctor, a petite Indian gentleman, ushered us into his kitchen where the evening meal was cooking on the stove.

He cleared plates and cups off the kitchen table, asked me to remove my underwear and said, "Sit on the table, please, so that I can take a look."

The expression on my face probably said more than any comment I could have come out with just then.

I looked at Jim. He said, "At least he's supposed to know what he's talking about. None of us know what to do."

True, having no other option, I sat on the table while the doctor took a look. The news was not good. It looked like I had been bitten by a fly that had burrowed under the skin and would probably lay eggs which would very quickly hatch and then eat their way out. These flies usually attacked cows and horses apparently. Great. The good news was that at least it was external. He could locate exactly where it was, cut it out, scrape out the eggs and I would be OK. If, on the other hand, it had entered my body, I might not have known it was there until it was too late. Still mentally digesting the good news, echoes of the 'cut it out and scrape out the eggs' comment were flashing horrific images through my mind. I went to climb off the table, expecting to have to travel to his clinic or hospital. He put out his hand to stop me.

"I can do it here," he said, then began to sort through what sounded like a cutlery drawer. *Are you kidding me?* I looked at Jim; he seemed uncertain too. By now the doctor was heading back towards me with what looked like a steak knife. Seeing my look of agitation, he tried to reassure me, saying, "It sounds worse than it is. It is only like lancing a boil really and you will feel so much better once it is done." *To you maybe it will only feel like lancing a boil.* I was certain that was NOT how it would feel to me.

Once again, he advanced, knife in hand, ready to get the job done. All I had to do was stay really still. He was starting to get a bit annoyed; this was clearly holding up his dinner, which did smell really good. Then, when I insisted that he sterilise the knife before he put it near any part of me, let alone down there, he realised he would have to do as I was asking if he was going to have any chance of getting rid of me. While he was sterilising the knife in some boiling water, Jim went outside to the car to let our friends know what was happening. They came into the house with Jim and said as long as I kept completely still it would be OK. They had seen it done before, although not in so intimate a place. The flies usually attacked animals. *Oh good! That is really reassuring. At least everyone seemed to be in agreement about what it was and how to deal with it. It did beg the question though, is this a doctor who usually deals with animals or humans?* Jim gave me a hug to try and reassure me, or so I thought, but in a split second, as the doctor took the knife out of the boiling water, Jim grabbed me around my arms. His friends grabbed a leg each and the doctor dived in to do his work. Damn! This was the second time in as many months that Jim had held me down against my will. We were going to have to have a serious talk about this. The knife, when it cut, was swift and decisive. It hurt like hell but the really excruciating pain was the scraping that followed to get all the eggs out. Job done at last, the doctor poured some alcohol over the cut. If I thought the scraping was bad, the alcohol nearly sent me through the roof. I screamed at this point. All done at last, the doctor rinsed the knife under the kitchen tap then popped it back in the cupboard drawer. They all released my arms and legs and I gingerly climbed off the kitchen table, cursing as I went. Although it still hurt like hell, it was beginning to feel better than it had done earlier, the swelling was going down noticeably. As we left the house, the doctor was just sitting down with his family at the kitchen table, ready to tuck into their delayed evening meal.

The next few days were interesting. Trying to use the toilet without feeling severe pain was not an option. I had an open cut, so pain was inevitable. However, trying to delay going only made it worse. The urine was stronger, it hurt more, so it worked out much better to drink a lot more water to weaken the urine and thus lessen the pain.

Slowly, oh so slowly, I began to heal. While I recovered, we spent our days sunbathing in the morning, resting in the afternoon, and then dinner in the restaurant in the evening. The original tourists had left now. Most of the groups only stayed two weeks and then went back home to various parts of the world so every fortnight or so we got a new group of people to entertain us and for Jim to entertain in return.

When I had fully recovered, we went on a safari, heading out at first light of dawn. Hard to describe how much brighter the light is here; you would have to visualise the brightest sunshine you have ever seen and then at least double it to even begin to imagine the intensity of the ochre colours of the landscape as the sun first hits them and then the optical illusion as that same sun warms the ground and a heat haze makes everything shimmer. It looks as though the ground itself is melting and evaporating into the air. The animals proved elusive, but we did see some lions and giraffes, although not close up.

Life at the hotel was relaxing and we had both needed that, but we were becoming restless now. Lack of activity was slowing us down. We needed some extra interests; we couldn't sunbathe forever. Jim heard about an Irish priest running a mission in the vicinity and decided to go and take a look. The drive was quite long and for a while we thought we might be lost but at last got there, although it was late in the afternoon by the time we arrived. We should have set off much earlier.

A journey that at home would have only been a few hours' duration had taken hours longer on these rough tracks. The priest was really interesting and invited us to stay the night; he would be glad of the company and to hear news from Ireland. We spent the evening listening to him telling us how he had arrived in Kenya and all the things he hoped to achieve, although with the trouble brewing in neighbouring Uganda, he wasn't sure how long he would be allowed to stay.

We told him all about Ireland. Things had been heating up there, too. We ended up spending the night in a mud hut. I kept all my clothes on, not willing to risk being bitten by anything again, although the mosquitoes that had been a real nuisance in the beginning seemed to have lost interest as I had become more tanned.

In the morning we got the guided tour of the mission and

the well they had dug, along with the pump the priest was trying to install. Lack of money as usual being a huge stumbling block to projects of this sort. Jim and I spent the day clearing scrub and helping connect the lengths of pipe that would eventually carry the water from the well to the mission buildings. We spent a second enjoyable evening in our mud hut and then headed back to our hotel the next morning. We hadn't expected to stay more than a few hours at the mission, so after two days we were seriously in need of a change of clothes. Jim had promised to help financially to finish the well project. That meant a trip to the bank in Mombasa to transfer the money. I decided to go along to do some shopping and see the sights, as long as it didn't include the rubbish dump. I had had enough of that on the way here. I hoped the road took a different route into Mombasa than the train did. The wife of one of Jim's friends agreed to take me to the shops while her husband took Jim to the bank.

There weren't really that many things that I wanted to buy, just some toiletries and some chocolate, that was about it. Shopping mission accomplished, my two or three parcels in my hand, I followed the friend's wife along the street to meet Jim and get a lift back to the hotel. A small boy only about five or six pulled at my arm, asking to carry my parcels.

I looked at him, saw how frail he looked and said, "No, thank you." I had seen children wherever we went walking behind white people carrying parcels, it always looked so terrible to me.

The wife stopped in her tracks, having heard this, looked

sternly at me and asked why I hadn't let him carry my parcels. I was dumbfounded. I protested, "But he's only a little boy. I would be so embarrassed to have such a tiny child walking behind me carrying parcels that I can carry myself."

She looked at me long and hard then said, "Why don't you stop thinking about how you would feel and think about him instead. He isn't begging, he is asking you to let him do a job so that he can earn some money and help to feed the rest of his family."

It would have hurt less if she had slapped my face as hard as she could. I was so shaken I just stood in the middle of the pavement, stunned, not sure what to do. But then the realization that I was still thinking about how I felt and not about the child. I felt a small tug at my sleeve. The same small boy waiting patiently. "Yes, please, I would like some help with my parcels," I said. It was a sobering experience and one that would remain with me for the rest of my life.

Jim loved the local fish at the restaurant each evening and decided that he would like to give fishing a go.

The fishing boats left early each morning. We were ready at the crack of dawn, having stayed up all night first watching the sun go down and then watching it come back up again; I couldn't decide which was the more beautiful. Finally I decided that dawn was the best as the sun came up over the ocean. The fish we were after was a marlin, a blue one, if possible, then you got to fly a flag on the back of your boat on the way back to the harbour to let everyone else know that you had caught one. We had a quick lesson from the crew as we sailed out about what to do with the rods should we get a decent bite and then we settled down to wait. Thankfully there was a decent canopy over the yacht. You couldn't walk on the decks without shoes by about ten o'clock, it was so hot.

We whiled away a few hours, watching the floats bobbing along behind the boat. Absolutely nothing happening. Jim got bored and went below to check out what was on offer for lunch.

I saw my float dip below the water then bob back up again. When it did it a second time, I grabbed the rod and tried to remember what I had been told to do. The reel was spinning out of control, had to stop that, but the little handle on the side of the rod was also spinning. I could barely catch hold of it, it kept smacking into my fingers. Why didn't they make it bigger?

In the end I had to call for help. One of the crew grabbed the rod, got it under control, then gave it back to me; so easy when you know how.

Two hours later I was still trying to reel it in, my whole-body aching, Jim feeding me sandwiches and drinks. I needed both hands for the rod. After three hours we could see the fish breaking the surface of the water, but it was still a long way from being landed. I had a blue marlin on my line. Now I was strapped into a harness to support my back and hold the rod in the front so that I didn't let go of it, then my harness was attached to the seat to stop me being dragged overboard.

This was seriously exhausting now, but after three and a half hours struggling, I wasn't going to give in to a fish, no matter how big it was.

I thought about the little blue marlin flag we would be able to fly from the back of the boat on the way back and the fish steaks we would have for dinner that evening. Then, after doing battle for just over four hours, the fish was half out of the water; one final haul should get it on board. The crew were standing ready to help me haul my fish on board. I let some slack on the fishing line, ready to reel in the last bit, when suddenly the whole thing went slack and I fell heavily back into my seat arms, my body shaking from my exertions. What the hell had happened? I looked at my fishing rod to see about two feet of marlin dangling off the end of my line. At the very last minute a shark had taken the rest of my fish. They let me fly the blue marlin flag on the way back, although to be fair we should really have flown it at half-mast. Once the head had been removed there was still enough left for some decent steaks, which the restaurant cooked for us that evening.

A chalet in the grounds had become available; we could move out of the flat and have a bit more privacy with our own enclosed garden. Jim was still suffering from a bit of hurt male pride. I had caught the blue marlin, not him. He was determined that he would catch one as well so while I moved our stuff, he was going fishing.

Moving only took a short time. We never had more than a suitcase each. Once done I settled down to read a book in our new outside space. It was cool under the overhanging shade trees and after an hour or so I dozed off, lulled asleep by the sound of the ocean only a few hundred yards away on the other side of the small wall that marked the end of the hotel grounds and the beginning of the beach. We never walked on the beach alone, only with a guard from the hotel. Although beautiful, it was also dangerous. Two tourists had been killed on the beach in the short time that we had been there; one stabbed, the other shot, both raped but ultimately killed for the small change they carried in their pockets.

I had no idea how long I had slept, maybe a few hours, but from the angle of the sun when I woke it was late afternoon. No sign of Jim, strange. I walked to the wall to see if there was any sign that the yacht had returned. It was anchored offshore, no signs of life on board. Maybe he had seen me asleep and decided to go to the bar. I checked the bar, then the restaurant.

The crew from the yacht were in the bar, still no sign of Jim, though. I thought I would just check our chalet again before saying anything to the crew. I felt a bit silly asking them where he was as though I were a suspicious wife checking up on an erring husband. Back at the chalet, still no sign of him and no indication that he had been there all day. I was beginning to get worried now. I would have to ask the crew. They looked surprised; said he hadn't been with them. Maybe he had gone out with one of the small local fishing boats. The yacht had been booked out all day with a tourist trip. Really worried now, I was just about to go back to the hotel to check again when I noticed a small sailing boat just mooring. Jim was easy to spot, and I watched as he strode proudly up the beach towards me, fish in hand. After the obligatory photographs, the proud angler, catch in hand, headed to the chalet. It was a nice fish but nowhere near as big as the one I had nearly landed. Would make another good dinner though. Jim was doing a strange walk. I hadn't noticed at first but now the nearer we got to the chalet, the worse it was becoming.

"What's wrong with your legs?" I said.

"It's not my legs," he replied. "It's my back."

"Why?" He had been out all afternoon on a small sailboat, no t-shirt, no sunscreen. His back was the colour of a cooked lobster. Blisters were beginning to form. Once inside the chalet he collapsed on his stomach on the bed, groaning. Within minutes his back looked like one huge blister. I grabbed ice from the fridge, put it on his back. He screamed in pain. The ice melted in seconds, virtually as soon as it hit his skin. I filled the bath with cold water and dumped in all the towels. Slowly I laid the first wet towel gently on the bottom of his back and kept on laying it bit by bit until he was covered up to his shoulders. It steamed as it hit his scorched skin, filling the bedroom with condensation. I could barely make out where the bed was anymore. By the time I had slowly reached the end of the towel, the beginning edge was dry. I ran to the bathroom for the next towel, taking the first towel with me to wet again. We had some painkillers. I gave him the maximum dose I could and continued with the towels. I tried putting them on faster, but his groans were so terrible even though he was biting on a pillow the whole time. I had to go slower. I kept thinking that he was going to pass out; it would have been easier to deal with if he had.

Hours passed. I was exhausted. I gave Jim more painkillers and the groans changed to low moans and eventually he slept, a fitfully sobbing fretful sleep. Was it him sobbing or me? I couldn't tell any more, I was so distressed that he was in such pain, and by trying to help him I had to add to that pain in the perhaps vain hope that it might make it better. I wondered if he was dreaming or if the pain was so great, he couldn't even do that.

At long last, after even more hours of trudging back and forth, there seemed to be signs of improvement. The condensation was beginning to clear; the towels were remaining wetter for longer and when I plucked up the courage to touch his back, it was getting cooler. The intense heat had given way to a more normal temperature, although when I removed my hand, I did expect half his back at least to come away on my hand.

I don't remember when I fell asleep but when I woke it was daylight outside. I was lying on the floor next to the bed. Jim was still sleeping. Not so fretful now but still clearly in pain; you could see it etched in his face and in the way his hands clenched and unclenched, still holding the pillow. Gingerly, I reached up to feel the towel that was still on his back: still damp. I sat on the floor next to him and cried quietly, partly relief, partly physical and mental exhaustion. I had been so scared last night. What if I had done the wrong thing, made it worse? What if he had become unconscious, then who would I have gone to for help?

The people Jim knew here did not even know our real names.

Jim was stirring now, slowly opening his eyes, the look of pain still there but not as acute as last night. I got up off the floor and carefully removed the towel from his back. His skin was red and wrinkled like someone who had stayed in the bath too long but much redder, but at least the skin was still there; although the blisters were so bad, I was certain he would lose most of it eventually. He tried to turn and sit up. The effort was too much. I had to help him, still crying at the sight of him so burnt.

He had the most beautiful skin, smooth and soft. Would it ever look that way again? Jim put it down to the buttermilk he had drunk as a child. I was trying to pull myself together. I didn't want him to see the state I was in and worry that he was worse than I was telling him. I was only fooling myself. He took a proper look at my face then forced himself off the bed, over to the mirror to see for himself. Looking at his back was difficult. His neck was burnt as well but he could see enough. I walked over to him and hugged his chest. He tried to hug me back but struggled with the effort of lifting his arms. We stood for a few moments locked in that strange half embrace. He apologised for all the times that he had sworn at me the previous night when I had been putting the towels on his back and what he had threatened to do to me as soon as he could get off the bed. I was sorry for some of the comments I had made to him about the stupidity of what he had done and the risks he had taken just to outdo me. We didn't need this in our relationship, he had enough of that nonsense within his own family. The responsibility of loving and caring for someone else so completely – a burden I hadn't expected, following on as it did from the joy and excitement of first love. Our African dream was tarnished now.

I murmured, "I want to go home." He gave the barest nod of his head in recognition that he had heard me; it was enough. We kept to our room for a few days. We both needed space to recover. I was glad that we were in the chalet. Jim's back was getting better but he was now minus a lot of skin so had to keep well covered to avoid infections. We sat in our outside space and read and talked. The days passed slowly but at least he was getting better. After about a week he felt well enough to venture down to the bar one evening. His back was still raw, he could barely stand to have anyone touch him. I had to time his painkillers to coincide with me changing his dressings. I was now counting the days until we could go back to Ireland but did not want to push him until he was fully recovered. It would be tough for him to sit for hours on a flight home until his back was more healed. There was another new group of tourists and this time there were some Irish ones as well and it didn't take long before Jim was chatting to them. At least it will take his mind off his back for a bit, I thought. All the talk seemed to be about Ireland and the recent events that had happened there. They asked us what we thought about what had happened.

What had happened? We didn't know.

They recounted the events of the previous few weeks, although their accounts varied slightly depending on which news items they had seen or which newspapers they had read. The basic facts seemed to be the same: a group of unarmed Irish people on a peace march in Belfast had been shot dead by the British army.

It would very quickly become known as Bloody Sunday.

Jim was beside himself; I had never seen him so angry. Back or no back, we were leaving on the next available flight.

But where would we go?

We had given up the house at Kilcoole, it would have to be a hotel for the time being or stay with friends.

The sensible option was to go back to Holland. Jim could carry on recovering there and get some proper medical attention, but the main advantage would be that he could find out about what was happening at home. The flight back was difficult. Jim was still in so much pain. All of the things that had excited me about the flight on the way out just seemed so inconsequential now on the way home and I took no interest in anything other than Jim. I must have looked the same as the other passengers who all tried to adopt the seen it all and done it all before attitude. Maybe I had become a jaded adult on our African adventure.

CHAPTER 8

Loosdrechtsedijk

Travelling continuously, although really exciting most of the time, does have its drawbacks. We were living out of suitcases all the time; not so bad when we were staying in hotels but when staying with friends or people Jim was doing business with, just the practicalities of getting laundry, etc. done could prove difficult.

We often stayed with Lucas and Sophie in their traditional old house in the south of Holland and heading there now was like a homecoming.

They had no indoor bathroom so having a wash involved stripping off in the kitchen. Everyone who visited them always entered the house through the kitchen door, which was usually unlocked so it was a unique way of making new friends.

The toilet was an interesting experience as well it was located in a shed behind the house across a path that ran behind the row of houses. Their house was the first house in that section of the street, so all the neighbours walked past their toilet first on their way home. The toilet door had no lock, just a cut-out shape to see through so that you could tell if the toilet was being used. This also took some getting used to. At first, I used to try and time any visits I needed to make but that wasn't always possible, so I just had to get used to it. I was used to outside toilets, a lot of my relatives had them, but they had always been located in the back yard of the house so had been reasonably private.

As Jim was becoming more involved with Howard, we were spending more time in Holland. We needed a proper place to stay, somewhere to leave things and just escape from it all every now and again and be able to spend time alone. We couldn't impose too much on Lucas and Sophie, although they were always pleased to have us, it didn't seem fair, and I worried that we would outstay our welcome and maybe lose some good friends in the process. I knew now from bitter experience what it felt like to be inundated with unwelcome guests. Jim agreed that we needed to find somewhere and preferably nearer Amsterdam. He needed to be able to get backwards and forwards to Ireland more easily.

Kilcoole had been our retreat in the beginning but when Howard came on the scene it quickly became a place of business with an endless stream of people coming to stay or trying to contact Jim at all hours of the day and night. We had ceased to get any peace there and, although I missed the house, I didn't miss that. Most of the problems had arisen because Howard and Jim had become such good friends. Previously business had always been kept away from our home and the only visitors had been Jim's family, our friends, and the random hitchhikers that Jim had brought home. As soon as Howard was on the scene, he brought an entire entourage with him who all seemed to feel that they could come and go as they pleased with little regard for the fact that this was our home, not a cheap hotel.

Jim began to search in Holland for somewhere to stay and found a flat in Loosdrechtsedijk, a village just south of Amsterdam. It was a small one-bed open-plan flat, too small for anyone to come and stay, thank goodness. Perfect.

The flat was in a small complex of two blocks of flats, each two storeys high. We had the flat on the upper floor, which although small was plenty big enough for just Jim and me. Some people had bought two flats, one above the other, and knocked through. The ground floor space at the end of our block housed a discotheque: The Pink Elephant. The other block at the opposite end to the discotheque housed a sauna. The two blocks faced each other, small gardens in front of the ground floor flats and some parking spaces separating the two. They were at right angles to the road and, apart from that connection to dry land, were completely surrounded by a lake.

We were close enough to Amsterdam to get there easily when we needed to but too far away for people to drop in unexpectedly. Even better. We settled in well, had fun looking for things for the flat, not that we needed much – it was already furnished, just a few personal things to make it our own – and got to know the neighbours. Our next-door neighbour, Elmo, worked at The Pink Elephant and we became regulars whenever we were in Holland. Jim had set up a company in Ireland selling business machines so in the main that was our cover story; we had to be able to explain our lifestyle without arousing suspicion.

One evening Jim had to meet Howard to discuss some business, it wouldn't take long he had said so I decided to go along as well. We were going to drive to Amsterdam and have a night out after their meeting. We dropped into The Pink Elephant for a quick drink before we set off. Elmo was in the bar and seeing Jim and I both dressed for a night out asked us where we were going. He then suggested a nightclub we should try so Jim invited him along as well.

We met Howard in the bar at The American hotel as arranged. One look at Howard was enough for Elmo to realise what Jim and Howard were actually doing in Holland and he was keen to be involved.

I sat with Elmo while Howard and Jim talked and then we all went to the nightclub that Elmo had suggested. Many hours and several clubs later we said goodbye to Howard and, minus Elmo who had got lucky and gone home with some guy he had met in one of the nightclubs, Jim and I made our way back to Loosdrechtsedijk.

Jim was unsure at first about having Elmo involved; he was living next door to us, too close to home, but the advantages outweighed the disadvantages. Elmo could speak Dutch and knew lots of good contacts or so he said – he was in.

The contrast between all of these lifestyles was astonishing. Just moving between Ireland and Holland was akin to visiting different planets or at the very least different centuries, but we glided between it all, adapting as we went to suit each environment and cover story. It had been so easy in the beginning, but now more and more people were becoming aware of what was going on. How long would it be before someone said the wrong thing to the wrong person?

My first trip to Holland had been a huge eye-opener; not so much the prostitutes in windows in the red-light district in Amsterdam, although it did surprise me that there were so many, but the products so openly on display in sex shop windows, even in small towns. How on earth did children react to this? It embarrassed me to see some of these things and I certainly did not wish to know what you were supposed to do with some of those contraptions. Likewise, their different views about drugs had also been an eye opener. In Ireland you could be falling down drunk most of your life and that was almost an acceptable way to be, mention smoking dope though and you brought down the wrath of God. In Holland cannabis was available in numerous places and although illegal seemed to be tolerated by most people. England had been somewhere in the middle of those two viewpoints when I left. Hippies had been making an appearance for some time now and their lifestyles were being if not accepted at least tolerated by a growing amount of people.

Sometime after our night out with Elmo and Howard, I began to get a strange sensation whenever I went out and I found it hard to shake the feeling that someone was watching us.

I'm not sure precisely when I began to feel that we were

being watched but it was a sensation that grew daily. Jim thought that I was getting paranoid and continually tried to laugh it off.

Until the day that we went to see a Dr Hook concert, then he had to take it seriously. Jim had brought Lucas and Sophie up to Amsterdam for the weekend to visit us.

Jim had arranged a hotel for them, and we had all had a great weekend. It was good to spend time with some real friends and repay them for all the times we had stayed at their place.

The final treat was the trip to the Dr Hook concert. The concert was in the south of Holland, and we were going to drop them off at home afterwards. Sophie and I were sitting in the back of the car, the boys sitting in the front, when looking out of the side window I saw a helicopter following the car. I watched it for about 15 minutes. It went out of sight every now and again but kept re-appearing. Sophie realised that I had stopped listening to her and was distracted by something outside the car and she leaned over and followed my gaze to try and see what I was looking at. She spotted the helicopter, too.

As the words "there's a helicopter following us" left my mouth, I already knew what Jim's reaction would be, but Sophie backed me up and said that she had seen it too and it did seem to be following the car. So, I carried on talking to Sophie and told her about the flat opposite ours where I was convinced people were watching us. I knew beyond a shadow of a doubt that when I went down to the Pink Elephant, or shopping, I was being followed. The hairs on the back of my neck and down my arms would become like an electric shock was passing through them, standing on end and so sensitive that the faintest breeze then sent shock waves through the rest of my body. I never saw anyone; I just knew beyond any doubt that they were there and watching me.

It had become so bad that I had stopped going out of the flat by myself, so inviting Lucas and Sophie for the weekend had been a good distraction. But now here we were again, and the watchers were still with us and were now pursuers but this time in a helicopter. Sophie was on my side and had a solution to the laughter from Jim who was telling Sophie to stop encouraging me in what he thought of as my imaginings. But Sophie had been watching the helicopter too and was at least open to the idea that it might in fact be following us.

We had plenty of time before the concert so she said to Jim to just turn off at the next town, drive around in a circle for a while and see if the helicopter is still above the car, then we would know if they had indeed followed us.

Half an hour later, having driven round in circles, Jim finally stopped the car in the centre of a small town, and we all got out of the car and stood and looked at the helicopter hovering in place above us. It stayed in place just long enough for us all to spot a guy with a camera taking photographs, then it sped away.

That wiped the smile off Jim's face. Not wishing to spoil

Lucas and Sophie's weekend, we carried on to the concert. Half an hour after arriving, Jim left us to enjoy ourselves, saying that he would pick us up later, take Lucas and Sophie home, and then we would talk. He was so on edge I was worried about him but at least he was listening to my concerns now.

The concert was really good. Lucas was in his element. Anything to do with bands plus a night out without having to worry about their two kids was all good.

We eventually dropped them off at home, declined the invite to stay until morning and decided instead to drive through the night straight back to the flat, arriving just before breakfast time.

Jim had calmed down a lot since the previous evening. I knew it couldn't have just been about the helicopter, I had been telling him about strange things going on for a few weeks now. Whatever he had been up to last night seemed to have gone well. I, on the other hand, was really annoyed with him. He had used our friends as a cover for something and I wasn't happy.

We argued about it, but he wouldn't tell me what he had been doing. I was angry because Lucas and Sophie were some of the few real friends that we had.

So many of the others who tried to get close to Jim were just hangers-on, trading on acquaintance with Jim and just out for what they could get, and they didn't seem too bothered about what they would have to do to get it.

Argument over, eventually we got around to talking about what I felt had been going on in the last few months, about the flat opposite and the feeling of being watched and followed when I went out. Jim said that the flat was empty, that it was up for sale. That begged the question, how would he know? He had to admit that he had been a bit worried about what I had been saying and had asked Elmo about the flat in the previous week. So much for telling me I was imagining things. Now, though, what were we going to do about it? We had been up all night and had been partying hard all weekend, we were exhausted and badly needed to sleep, but we even more urgently needed to know what was going on in the flat opposite. Jim spoke for both of us when he suggested we go take a look.

We walked over to the other block. The doors to the flats were at the rear of the property, accessed by an exterior flight of stairs and walkway that ran the whole length of the block. It was the middle of the morning by now. Most of the neighbours would be at work. We identified the flat, which did to all outward appearances seem to be empty, and Jim booted the door open. The place was deserted except for a selection of takeaway cartons and drinks cups scattered on the floor in front of the window that faced our flat. Someone or several someone's had clearly spent a good deal of time by that window.

As casually as possible, in case anyone was in and had heard the door being kicked in, we strolled back to our flat and went to bed.

There was no denying it now, we were being watched and almost certainly followed as well, and not just by the helicopter last night. We would have to look at every aspect of our lives now and who we were associating with and why.

What had started out as a small venture with Howard was now completely out of control and growing by the day.

People who would never have been anywhere near us in the past were now staying in our houses and invading our lives.

When I had first become involved with Jim, he was surrounded by family and friends he had known for years. He trusted these people with his life and with mine.

Now we seemed to be surrounded by people we barely knew and trusted even less.

Being friendly with our neighbour Elmo had brought certain benefits but it had also brought its own set of problems as well.

Whenever we went to The Pink Elephant club, we were surrounded by a group of hangers-on who all wanted to be part of the in-crowd as they now seemed to view us.

One girl in particular had her eye on Jim and wasted no time in making her intentions known. Zoë was a friend of Elmo's, so it was very difficult for me to try and exclude her from our group. Much though I wanted to, I was uncertain how I should deal with this. She was breathtakingly beautiful with long, blonde hair and eyes the colour of the

Mediterranean Sea, plus a stunning figure, and although I really liked her, I also felt threatened by her and the interest that Jim showed in her.

Now I just wanted to get away from everything, all the hangers-on and the however many people who were following and watching us – I wondered if they had bugged the flat; were they listening when we were in bed together? And of course, Zoë and all the other girls who constantly tried to catch Jim's eye. But most of all I wanted to be away from the situation that now required us to have the gun that Jim now carried in the glove box of the car every time we left the flat.

I seemed to be worrying about everything now, things were out of Jim's control and getting more so every day. I had almost felt safer in Belfast, at least we knew who our enemies were there.

The chance to get away from it all for a while and have a change of scene came from an unlikely source, we did talk about whether or not it was a good idea but in the end Jim accepted.

CHAPTER 9

Ibiza

Howard had rented a house on the island of Ibiza for the summer.

Jim and I were invited to stay as long as we wanted.

Sunshine was always good, but I wasn't sure how I would get on in close proximity to Howard's wife. The only time I had met her previously she had virtually thrown me out of their house and then she and Howard had a huge argument because Howard had insisted that I stay. Howard was always staying at our house in Kilcoole, he wasn't going to put me in a hotel when I was in England.

He had won that particular argument and, after some heated discussion, I had reluctantly agreed to spend the night at their house, but it was difficult and uncomfortable, and I had been glad to leave as soon as possible. Jim had been keen that I should go to Oxford to see Howard's business. He couldn't come to England himself and wanted to see what my opinion would be.

Howard had been staying at our house for a few weeks and when he knew that he was going back home he had invited me to Oxford for a few days before I continued on to Holland.

We arrived at his house early evening. His wife hit the roof the second we walked through the door. "What the hell is she doing here?" *Nice greeting*, I thought, *who does she think I am*. Even after Howard introduced me, there was still no let up. He hustled me into the spare room, clearly embarrassed but insisting that I stay.

He had stayed at our house on so many occasions, always welcomed. Jim and I both enjoyed his company; I couldn't understand what was going on. Jim wouldn't be a happy man if I told him about this. He valued hospitality and always tried to make everyone feel at home when they stayed with us.

Morning did not appear to have improved the situation. Howard got me out of the house as soon as possible. I made sure that I had my suitcase with me. There was no way I was going to spend another night at Howard's house.

I was staying in a hotel until my flight to Holland the following day. We went to Howard's shop, a small boutique in Oxford. I resisted the urge to fill another suitcase, though there were some very nice clothes. I booked into a hotel and Howard went home to face the music. I didn't find out what Howard's wife's problem was with me until sometime later.

Howard had apparently been seeing someone else and his wife thought that Jim and I knew about it and had been covering for him. We didn't know about it and had no idea who he had been seeing or when. The damage had been done though; we would never get on. She was always hostile after that. If she phoned our house in Kilcoole to speak to Howard and I answered, there would be no conversation, just "Get Howard, it's his wife."

Ibiza should be interesting.

We had been invited for as long as we wanted, although Jim would still have to come and go, as would Howard. Business would have to continue as usual. I didn't fancy the prospect of being left alone with Howard's wife but other people had been invited, including some friends from Holland. The only fly in the ointment – someone had invited Zoë.

From the first moment that we had met Zoë, she had made a bee line for Jim. He was interested, hard not to be, Zoë was very beautiful, but for the moment he was behaving himself. Zoë came out to Ibiza for a few weeks but during her stay she started seeing one of the other husbands and after a huge row with the man's wife one night, she went back to Holland.

The house Howard had rented was just outside the main tourist area near the old medina of Ibiza. When Jim wasn't around, I would wander for hours around the narrow streets looking at the little market stalls: fresh fish, vegetables, and handmade jewellery.

My favourite, though, was the stall that sold wooden board games, especially the chess boards: mahogany and exotic woods and ivory all banded together in intricate patterns – the hours it must have taken to make those boards.

Tourists came in their droves to Ibiza town, not only for the sunshine but for the fantastic nightlife. There were nightclubs everywhere.

It was as much fun to sit in the cafes along the route to the clubs and watch the nightly parade of partygoers dressed in their most outrageous outfits as it was to go to some of the clubs.

The seafront promenade provided the perfect catwalk for the preening partygoers. The really good outfits would receive a small ripple of applause as they progressed along the route, like a Mexican wave slightly preceding them. By the noise volume generated you knew when to look up from your meal and see if you agreed with the public's decision.

Jim and I went to the clubs occasionally but mainly preferred more off-the–beaten-track places where you could still hear yourself speak. We both loved Ibiza though and wanted to stay as long as possible.

Things were no better with Howard's wife so, when Jim wasn't around, I just kept out of her way as much as possible.

Howard had brought a nanny to look after his children and we became friendly so when she wasn't working, we would hang out together. It was good to have a female friend nearer my own age.

Rachel, the nanny, was good fun and we got on well together; she appreciated my company as much as I appreciated hers and we had some great nights out together. At the house though an old familiar pattern began to emerge that I remembered so well from the gruesome twosome. When Jim and Howard were around, Howard's wife was barely civil, just enough to prevent all-out war.

As soon as they were gone, hostilities resumed. I loved Ibiza but didn't want to spend any longer than I absolutely had to in this house. Rachel and I would go out exploring as much as possible up into the old town, where I showed her all the places I had found, or out into the country around Ibiza town.

One day we spotted a small house with a 'for rent' sign. I took down the number and rang that evening. The house was for rent for the rest of the summer. Without even making an appointment to view the inside of the house I took it.

Basic was probably a kind description of the house and its lack of facilities, no running water, only an outside well set into the front of the house which did have water, no electricity, furniture, kitchen or bathroom. The main thing in its favour was it did have walls and a roof and a door. Most importantly though it had a small, isolated beach within walking distance from the house, down a narrow sandy path. We could do whatever we wanted here; there was no one else around for miles.

In town, Rachel and I bought some large pieces of foam for mattresses and some sheets. A camping stove and small barbeque would have to do for cooking food. I also bought a spade; we were going to have to dig a few holes outside. There was no point in buying loads of stuff for only a few months. Half the time we went out for dinner anyway, so we just got the necessities and considered staying at the house was just like camping. Rachel was still working so couldn't stay at the house overnight, she had to be around in the morning to make the children's breakfast etc, so I moved into the house on my own. It was a bit scary at first being there all alone, especially at night, and if I needed the toilet wandering around in the dark hearing strange noises in the undergrowth could be pretty alarming, but I soon grew to love it.

Rachel came around when she could to keep me company and it wouldn't be long until Jim was back.

Jim was back at last, and he loved the house too. We spent a beautiful couple of weeks together, swimming each day then walking back to the house to barbeque our evening meal and watch the sun go down. So far only the three of us had been there. Jim and I had managed to keep the house pretty much to ourselves with only an occasional visit from Rachel, but now as the summer was coming to an end he asked for a favour.

Jim had seen Lucas and Sophie while he had been in Holland. They were going through a tough time, and he asked if I minded if he invited them to stay with us for a holiday.

I loved them both and their children so of course not.

We had stayed with them so many times it was only fair, although I would miss being alone with Jim.

They came over for the last two weeks of the summer; it was good to have such good friends around, although I was sad that they were having problems and hoped that the holiday would maybe give them a chance to sort it out.

The days were long and leisurely. As Jim and I had done previously, we all strolled to the beach each day, swam, and sunbathed then strolled back to the house and spent the evening sitting outside under the stars, whiling away the time chatting and enjoying the odd glass or two of alcohol.

The days were so quiet and peaceful, just the sounds of the sea and insects buzzing about only interrupted by weird singing to inform people of their whereabouts if anyone had gone for a walk in the bush with the spade.

Summer was nearly over, it was time for everyone to go home, so I decided to throw a leaving party. Rachel helped me.

We organised a feast at the house. A local restaurant would supply the roasted meat, then Rachel and I did all the salads and olives, breads, and local wines.

We spent a day with a craft knife cutting out letters from large leaves to make into party invitations and invited Howard and anyone who was staying at his house who wanted to come to the party.

We used our foam beds as couches for people to lie on and leaves were spread on the floor to lay out the food. We didn't have enough plates or glasses either, so everyone ate with their hands and drank straight from the bottles, nobody seemed to mind.

Chatting to a few Dutch people who had come with Howard, one of them mentioned it was a shame that Zoë had felt unwell and hadn't come to the party. Zoë … it couldn't be the same one surely, she had gone home weeks ago.

The party went on for several days. Rachel and I went out a couple of times to get more food and I had the chance to ask her about Zoë. "Yes it was the same one, she had come back a week ago." Rachel had no idea why. I had a pretty fair idea.

Jim was due to go back to Holland and was taking the same flight back as Lucas, Sophie, and the children.

Rachel and I took them all to the airport. I wasn't at all pleased to see Zoë turn up to take the same flight.

Jim would be in Holland on his own, I wouldn't be back for another week, I had to sort out closing the house and returning the keys plus paying the final bills.

I fretted the whole time just wanting to be with him, unsure how I should react to the whole Zoë situation. She was clearly out to get him; I had no clue how to deal with that.

He had asked me to marry him, we were engaged, that should have been a "No, No" to Zoë but apparently wasn't.

Where did I go from here?

Rachel was as astounded as I was. She had had no idea why Zoë had come back and was surprised when I had said that I thought Zoë was after Jim. She could offer no real solution. Maybe I should just get on a plane early and go and see what was happening.

I had never mistrusted Jim before and didn't want to start now but jealousy was getting a grip on me. I would have to do something. Jim had never been an angel in the time we had been together, but he had always been honest, even on the occasions when he knew I wouldn't want to hear what he had to say.

Then, unexpectedly, he came back to Ibiza with some more people in tow.

Our house was closed up and I had given back the keys, so we stayed at Howard's. Howard and his family had already gone back to Oxford, just leaving Rachel behind to close up the house.

Jim seemed OK but something had changed, he was trying too hard around me. With these new guests to keep entertained we had no real chance to talk. I would have to bide my time. We were going home in a few days, then I could get a better idea about what had happened, if anything, between Jim and Zoë.

On our last evening I sat on the doorstep of the house looking at the stars, the sky so clear here I thought I could see forever. One large bright star caught my eye, with two smaller stars blinking, one either side of it. Fancifully the large star I imagined was Jim, one of the smaller stars was me, the other Zoë. I became engrossed with watching these three stars. They were like Morse code signalling a secret message to me.

My small star blinked brightest for a while, the other one on and off for a while, then it stabilised and stopped blinking, maintaining a strong light. I waited for it to fade again but it didn't. Mine, on the other hand, having started brighter, had begun to blink more and was now less visible and had at last paled to almost nothing, only an occasional blink to let you know it was still there in the background, but only just.

Was that going to be my fate? I was heartbroken. Jim had come out to find me. I was still looking at the stars, a few tears running down my cheeks.

He thought I was upset about leaving and sat quietly cuddling me. I wanted to scream at him "what's going on between you and Zoë?", but I couldn't find the words. If I accused him and it wasn't true, he would know that I had doubted him. Our whole relationship was based on trust. If we trusted no-one else, we had to at least trust each other.

I couldn't bring myself to tell him about the stars. It was too painful to think about, let alone try and talk about. He would never understand what I was trying to tell him, that it was all about my insecurity about him and Zoë.

It felt too superstitious, even to me when I thought about it, but I knew my premonition was right.

Ever since that weird experience in Kerry, I had seemed to sense things differently, especially when it was things that concerned Jim. I had no idea why these apparently random things had such a hold over me or why I paid them so much attention. At times it fascinated me, at other times it seemed quite scary but on nearly every occasion at least some part of what I had been feeling had proved to be right.

We left Ibiza the following day as planned.

CHAPTER 10

Untersuchungshaftanstalt

If only I had paid more attention to those stars, I might not be in the situation I now found myself in.

I had been arrested in Hamburg a few weeks earlier and was now languishing in their category A prison accommodation awaiting my fate.

Nothing had happened for several days now. The cell door remained closed, only the hatch in the door opened three times a day and a bowl of food and a plastic cup of drink was passed through.

The guards or warders, I had no clue what to call them, occasionally said something to me in German, which I couldn't understand, then they closed the hatch, and I didn't see them again until the next mealtime.

The food bowl was china and about the size of a small mixing bowl. All the meals were put into this bowl with a metal spoon to eat with. Breakfast was usually bread in the bowl and coffee, which also went in the bowl.

Lunch, the main meal, was usually meat of some sort in gravy. I could never be sure what sort of meat it was, best not to know probably, then mashed potatoes plus vegetables all in sauces that mixed together and turned various strange colours with a really unappetising smell, it reminded me of Bray all those years before.

The last meal of the day was usually bread and coffee again with jam or sometimes cold meat. I had started throwing the food down the toilet. I could not face eating it. The only time I had passed the bowl through the hatch with food still in it, the guards had simply piled the next meal on top of the cold leftovers and passed it back to me. I sometimes managed to eat some bread, but my appetite had gone.

Sitting doing nothing all day, I did not feel hungry. I looked around at the things in my cell and went through the list: a bed, with a mattress and blanket, no sheets; one pillow, no pillowcase; a chair, a toilet, a sink. I used to try and keep occupied by putting this meagre list in different order then closing my eyes and trying to remember the correct order for each list. Largest item first, smallest item first, palest colour first etc, but after a very short time I had run out of categories. There was also a makeshift table that consisted of a piece of wood that you suspended from chains on the wall, and I thought, not for the first time, of all the rooms I had stayed in over the last few years. I remembered them with similar lists where had I been happiest, where had I been saddest, where had I been loneliest etc. but where I was right now was on every sad, lonely, miserable level the worst place I had ever been in my life and I had no way of knowing how long I would have to be here.

When I left my home to be with Jim I had only the clothes I stood up in. Now here I was again with just what I was wearing: a skirt, a blouse, a cardigan, tights, and my underwear. I had been trying to keep track of the time I had been here; I thought about six weeks. But I had no way of knowing with any real accuracy. I had nothing to write with or any books to read and I had been wearing these same clothes all that time. In the beginning I tried to wash my underwear every day, but cold water and a small bar of cheap hand soap did not do a very good job. I tried to wash myself, but the weather was getting colder now. I figured it was about mid-November. There was no heating in the cell or hot water, and when I undressed to try and wash with cold water, I had no towel to dry myself or my hair so day by day I was getting dirtier and smellier. Having no toothbrush or toothpaste my mouth felt horrible and that was adding to my lack of appetite as well.

I tried not to think about it.

I was sleeping more during the day now; it was warmer than at night, when trying to sleep in my clothes with only one blanket and the temperate only just above zero was impossible.

At night I walked about more: three steps one way, four the other. Time seemed to pass more quickly in the dark, thinking about nothing. During the day, time was broken up into segments of different activities going on somewhere else in the prison. I could hear cell doors opening below me, people moving about inside and outside but I couldn't see anything out of the cell window, it was too high up, my only view was of a small piece of sky and a watchtower with an armed guard.

Sometimes I heard voices wafting up from outside. It seemed to be some kind of exercise yard below my window, but it sounded quite a long way down.

I wondered what they did the rest of the day. Were they allowed books or newspapers? Were they allowed to speak to other people?

Did they do any work in the prison?

How long would they leave me in here completely alone with absolutely nothing to do all day? How long would I be able to stand this total isolation? If I had ever imagined prison, this was nothing at all like I had thought it would be.

Would I see a lawyer anytime soon or be able to speak to someone who spoke English, at least even if only for a few moments?

I wondered what was happening with Elmo. Was he in this prison or had they taken him somewhere else?

He had been arrested at the same time as me. Were they treating him as badly as they were treating me? I had re-lived what had happened over and over in my mind. Jim must know where I was by now.

Why was nothing happening?

Elmo and I had come to Hamburg together to pick up a car that had been left in a multi-story car park. The driver had panicked, thought he was being followed and had ditched the car with 120 kilos of cannabis in the boot. It had to be moved before the police or anyone else found it.

We were in Holland when the phone call to Jim had found us. There never seemed to be any peace these days. The cars had all left Ireland and were being delivered all over Europe. If one car was caught all the others would be at risk. Elmo was the only person available to go and collect the ditched vehicle but felt that, if he went alone, it would be more suspicious than if a couple were in the car together, and so at the very last minute I had agreed to go with him, there was no one else we could trust.

Jim was very reluctant at first. I had never been involved in any of this business before, but he had things to do that night and it was urgent; there was no time to argue or to make any other plans.

Jim drove Elmo and me to the airport with only minutes to spare before the last flight that evening to Hamburg. As they rushed us through the gates, I turned to kiss Jim goodbye. He kissed my cheek and said, "See you in a few days," and turned to leave, his mind on other things now.

He did not hear me asking him to kiss me properly as he quickly walked away.

I watched him as long as I could whilst being hustled through the passport checks by Elmo. A cold hard circle of metal was fastening around my heart, getting tighter by the second. It felt like I was about to have a heart attack. I just knew I would not be seeing Jim in those promised few days and my chance to say a proper goodbye to him had gone.

On the plane Elmo thought fright had set in but I told him about the feeling of dread that had just enveloped me in the airport. He tried to reassure me that it was just nerves. I remembered Kerry and knew it wasn't, but we were nearly on our way now so there was no turning back. Elmo tried to cheer me up, he knew it was my birthday soon; we would be back by then and he knew what Jim had planned.

I knew that Elmo was nervous himself, so I tried to be as calm as possible on the flight.

We were taking off so definitely no second thoughts now about what we were going to do; we were on our way.

We took a taxi from the airport to the Atlantic hotel in the middle of Hamburg and booked a double room.

We had some dinner together and then went to look for the car park and check out the car. The car park was walking distance. We found it easily and started to look for the car.

We located it a few floors up; Elmo unlocked the boot, checked the contents, and then locked it again. Everything appeared to be OK, we couldn't see anyone watching the car and no-one challenged Elmo when he opened the boot.

We would come back and move it in the morning. We walked back to the hotel, feeling relieved and reasonably confident that things were OK.

Jim rang just as we got back to the room. He gave Elmo

all the details about where to go the following day and then he and I chatted for about half an hour.

Elmo went out for a drink to the bar while I was chatting to Jim. I told Jim about my feelings of dread at the airport. He was worried but tried to sound upbeat.

It was not the first time I had felt strange things and I had been right in the past as I reminded him. This was not helping either of us, so I changed the subject and tried to get him to tell me what he had planned for my birthday. No joy with that, he wouldn't even give me any clues.

He was out that night but would not tell me what he was doing. I just knew from his whole manner and the edge to his voice that it was something big. He would usually tell me afterwards, then if anything went wrong nobody could blame me or say that I was an informant, which in Belfast would have been my death sentence.

He had to go. We said goodnight.

I put the phone down and felt the circle of metal around my heart tighten again.

Elmo was still not back so I had a shower and went to bed. I hoped he was not going to come back drunk and wake me up. We had a lot to do the following day.

Next morning, no Elmo, no message, nothing. Where the hell was he?

I packed my suitcase, just leaving out the clothes I was going to wear that day and decided to have a soak in the bath to pass a bit of time until we were going to move the car.

No doubt he would turn up eventually.

He had probably picked up some guy in the bar and ended up in another room in the hotel.

As I was getting out of the bath, there was a loud knock at the bedroom door. Elmo must have forgotten his key.

I wrapped a towel around myself and went to open the door.

As I turned the handle, the door was thrust open violently, pushing me backwards into the bedroom. I had no option but to move backwards with it to avoid being jammed against the wall.

I felt a sharp pain in the centre of my head, right between my eyes, and felt rather than saw that a gun was now pressed against my forehead.

As I tried to focus on the gun, I was also aware of the man who was holding it and now forcing me back along the hallway. He was approximately the same height as Jim with the same dark hair and build but, unlike Jim who had dark eyes, this man had the most amazing pale blue eyes. I put his age as mid-forties. There was another man stood a little further behind, he was also well built and of a similar age as the first man. He also had a gun and, as we passed the bathroom door, he darted in quickly and just as quickly came back out and followed us into the bedroom.

Neither of them said a word. My mind was racing. I had

no idea who these men were. Maybe police, maybe local drug dealers. The initial fright on opening the door and having a gun pressed against my head had been replaced by an unnatural calm.

I had no choice in the matter anyway, the gun was still against my head although not pressed quite so hard now. I would just have to wait and see what was going to happen, in the meantime I just had to go where they were pushing me.

We were in the bedroom now. The second man had darted in ahead of us as the corridor opened into the bedroom and had checked the room and the wardrobe, spotting my packed suitcase on the bed. He had quickly rifled through it.

Finding that I was alone in the room and appeared to be unarmed, they both visibly relaxed. The gun to my head was put down a little and first man said something in German to the second man. The first man seemed to be in charge. I stood waiting, feeling vulnerable standing in a room with two men with guns. Wrapped only in a bath towel, I wondered who they had expected to find with me, possibly Jim, or did they know that I was here with Elmo?

I thought what would happen if Elmo suddenly walked into the room, or the maid. Would they panic and shoot me?

The two men carried on their conversation. They appeared to be trying to decide what to do. They had clearly not expected to find me on my own, if they had expected to find me at all.

The second man picked up the clothes that I had left on

the bed, pushed them towards me and made gestures to say that I should put them on.

I turned to head towards the bathroom. In that instant the gun was against my head again and the second man jumped in front of me to block my exit from the bedroom.

The first man was speaking to me in German. I stood looking at him then looked down the length of the barrel again, up the whole length of his arm, and finally into those beautiful blue eyes and said as slowly and calmly as I could, "I do not speak German." He eased up again but by gestures made it clear that I had to dress in the bedroom. As he lowered the gun, I slowly turned my back towards them both and started to get dressed, still trying to hold the bath towel around me. While I was putting my clothes on, the second man closed my suitcase. As soon as I was dressed, the second man picked up my handbag and, with the first man in front of me, he took up the rear and we all left the room. They both put their guns away as we all walked through reception. We all stopped while both men spoke to the receptionist, the second man then took money from my handbag to pay the bill. I was feeling pretty confident at this point that these two were police.

This was all so surreal, it felt as though I was in the middle of some strange dream that I would wake up from at any moment.

As we left the hotel, a car pulled up outside. It was a small two-door car, a bit beaten up surely this couldn't be a police car. The first man stepped forwards, opened the passenger door, pulled the passenger seat forwards and started to push me into the back of the car. I only got a passing glance at the driver as I fell face first into the back of the car. He seemed to be a similar sort to the other two. I struggled to right myself and turn around in the confined space in the back of this small vehicle.

My calm was beginning to wear off now. I was doubting my initial thoughts that they were police, and this was definitely no dream. What if they were drug dealers, something had gone wrong, and they were taking me as a hostage, or worse they were just going to kill me?

I thought about shouting for help. There were people walking by on the pavement but what could I shout? I didn't know any German, let alone the German for "Help, I'm being abducted by two gun-wielding maniacs." As I sat up, I saw the second man, with my suitcase and handbag, walk behind the car. I could hear another car pulling up behind us. I heard a door open and close. I assumed he had gotten into the other car.

We drove through the streets of Hamburg. I had not seen it in daylight before.

The roads were busy, people going about their normal daily lives, while I was in a car with two strangers with another car behind being driven to an unknown destination.

I sat in the back of the car wondering what I should do, but apart from watching the busy streets go by, there was nothing I could do.

The car was being driven by the third man, I had a better chance to look at him now. He did indeed match the first two, short, tidy hair, almost military haircuts. They had to be police, that was all I could think about as the city streets passed by.

At least that meant I was fairly safe.

Have they got Elmo, I wondered, *or Jim?*

The car slowed and turned under an archway and through a large set of doors into what appeared to be a large government building. The doors closed behind us, and we came to a stop in a courtyard in front of another set of doors.

Man number one jumped out, moved the passenger seat forwards and took my arm to get me out of the car.

Still holding my arm in a firm grip, he propelled me roughly through the doors, which had opened as we drew up outside, and then into the building. We moved along through three or four corridors of what looked like offices and into an empty room and stood waiting. For what?

Who knew, certainly not me? He didn't speak English and I didn't speak any German, maybe we were waiting for an interpreter.

He didn't release the firm grip on my arm and we both stood in this empty room, frozen in time as the minutes ticked by.

I glanced at him.

He was quite a handsome man; under different circumstances I would have found him really attractive.

I wondered what he was thinking as we stood there.

He was probably relieved that it had all happened so peacefully.

It must be pretty nerve-wracking to knock on a hotel bedroom door, not knowing what you will find waiting for you behind it.

After what seemed like an eternity but was probably only about five minutes, I heard footsteps in the corridor outside. The door opened and a stern-looking woman in what looked like a police uniform came into the room, said something in German to the first man and we were on the move again, this time to another office with a table with chairs on either side of it. Man number one plus the woman sat down on one side of the table and motioned to me to sit down on the other side. A minute later we were joined by man number two with my suitcase and handbag, which he put on the table between us.

All three of them then began a meticulous search of my suitcase and belongings, the woman making written notes and occasionally making comments, which I of course couldn't understand, to the two men.

It was a very odd situation to sit watching strangers minutely examine my underwear, especially as there was also the clothes that I had worn the previous day in the suitcase.

They seemed to be making a note of where the clothes

had been bought as they carefully checked all the labels as well.

The linings of the suitcase were also thoroughly examined, as were the contents of my makeup bag and handbag. Seemingly satisfied with the search, they put everything they had removed back into the suitcase and the woman officer left the room with it, leaving only my handbag on the table, the contents spread out before us all.

I looked down at my passport and the return ticket for later that day and wondered if they knew who I really was. I knew the cover story I was supposed to tell in case of a situation like this. It was the same for everyone. All I had to do was stick to the story for as long as possible to give the others as much time as possible to get away.

Jim would know by early that evening that something was wrong if he had not heard from me as arranged. I thought they must have arrested Elmo, that was why he had not returned to the hotel, so now I would just stick to the story and wait to see what would happen. The two male officers sat looking at me, expressionless.

We once again appeared to be waiting for something, but what?

Eventually the door opened, and a small middle-aged man entered the room. He came to my side of the table, extended his hand to shake mine and said in reasonable English, "I have been appointed by the police to interpret some questions they are going to put to you." And so, the questioning began. The day passed at a snail's pace, the same questions from them over and over again, the same answers from me over and over again. I tried several times to ask the interpreter questions – could I speak with a lawyer, could someone tell me my rights here in Germany – he steadfastly refused to answer any of my questions, and I had no idea if he had translated my questions to the police officers in the room with us.

Hours later I had stuck to my story whilst it had gradually grown dark outside.

I knew that Jim would definitely know by now that something had gone wrong.

I barely listened to the translated questions now and spent my time wondering what Jim was doing and imagining the frenzied phone calls that would be going back and forth.

Exhaustion was setting in, and I realised that I had not eaten or drunk anything all day. My last meal had been the previous evening. The police officers seemed to sense this as well. They were getting nowhere; we were just going round in circles now.

The questions stopped and I was taken from the room down another series of corridors until a final door opened into what was clearly a prison.

It was a large, vaulted room with rows of cell doors on two floors either side of the room.

Over the central aisle was netting which I presumed was

to stop people from jumping from the top floor or throwing things onto people walking below. This netting also covered the staircases, one at each end of the room. I was hustled quickly through this room into another similar room and then on into a third, this one with female prison officers, unlike the previous two which had appeared to only contain male officers.

I had never thought about prisons being connected to police stations before or, for that matter, court houses, which as I was later to find out, was also in this same building.

The wardress that I had been handed over to took me to a cell with a bath in it and indicated to me that I should get in it.

Naively I stood and waited for her to leave the room and then for the second time in 24 hours I realized that I had to stand and undress in front of a complete stranger.

After my bath I was escorted to yet another room where a queue of noisy women was lined up in what looked like a doctor's surgery. No one took any notice of me as I joined the end of the queue, and I was glad of a few minutes peace to look around. I glanced at the women in front of me, compared to them I was incredibly overdressed.

Flesh of all descriptions hung out of clothing that fitted where it touched and then only just. Underwear seemed to be an alien concept to most of them. The most covered parts of their bodies were their faces by makeup, which in the harsh neon lights of the prison was scary.

I dreaded to think what they looked like in daylight or if they ever went out when the sun was up.

As the queue advanced and we all got further into the room, I became aware of what was happening. The women at the front of the queue were being given what looked like bedpans and were then squatting and urinating into them. As I reached the front of the queue, they tried to hand me a bed pan, but I refused to take it.

A buzz of interest crept around the room and the chattering slowly stopped.

Now they were interested. The wardress tried several times to make me take the bedpan, I just ignored her.

It was a stalemate between the wardress and me.

I had no clue about my rights to refuse in this situation but couldn't see how they would be able to force me so I stood my ground, kept my hands at my side and said "NO" in the sternest voice I could manage.

She met my gaze for a moment then looked away, wrote something on her chart and gestured for me to move on.

The next indignity was the couch with the legs in the air for the internal examination in full view of everyone else. From the looks of a lot of the women here that would have been just another day at the office.

Again, my answer was "NO". Emphatically "NO". The wardress's looked perplexed, but what could they do about it? There were only three women officers in the room, and it would take more than that if they were going to try and force me.

The stalemate was broken again by a look away and a note on the chart.

I was then bundled out of the room and after a march along several corridors and up several flights of stairs, I was led into a cell in the middle of the corridor where the door was slammed behind me, and I was left alone.

I slept only occasionally throughout that long night. My mind was in total turmoil. I was so hungry and in such strange surroundings having no idea what was going to happen to me I just hoped Jim was safe.

As dawn came in through the window, I gave up all pretence of sleeping and paced the cell. Still no peace; I could hear a long series of cell doors above and below being opened and then slammed shut, none of them sounded close to mine though and I wondered who was in the cells either side of me.

Suddenly my cell door opened. In front of me was a trolley with coffee and bread and a bored-looking woman in a prison uniform accompanied by a guard. I indicated my preference with a series of gestures. I was glad of the food and drink, I couldn't remember the last time I had had either. Then without a word being spoken by any of us, the door was closed, and it was the turn of the next cell, which sounded as though it was at the very end of the corridor; it appeared as though I had no immediate neighbours.

Later that morning my cell door opened again, and I was

walked back through the series of corridors I had walked through the previous day and returned to the police office.

Different interpreter this time, same policemen, and we all spent another day going over the same questions time and time again with me giving the same answers time and time again.

At least this time they thought about feeding me and a sandwich was brought for me, I guessed, in about the middle of the afternoon. *When did they all eat*, I wondered?

Early that evening, both policemen stood up at the same time and one of them began a long monologue, the gist of it being that I was being charged and that I would be held in prison until my trial date, without bail, according to my interpreter.

I thought for a minute and then said, "Sorry, I must have been asleep when we went before the judge with my lawyer and my bail was denied."

The interpreter translated this to the two police officers, they just shrugged their shoulders and left the room. A uniformed policeman entered the room, and I was escorted back to the prison wing; this time, though, to the cell that I was currently occupying.

Over the course of the next few weeks, I was questioned on many occasions with many different interpreters, and I now began each session with the same questions: When will I get my lawyer? When will my trial be? I want to speak to the consulate.

Each time the questions were translated into German and each time they were ignored. It was extremely monotonous but at least I was out of the cell for a few hours.

But now nothing was happening.

My cell door hadn't opened in weeks, the hatch in the door opened three times a day and food was passed through, other than those few seconds of contact each day I spent the rest of the time totally alone.

I used to pace the cell and count the bricks in the wall, divide that by the number of tiles on the floor, multiply them together and then start again.

I now understood well the expressions 'cabin fever' and 'stir crazy'. Maybe I could come up with my own expression for this unique situation I found myself in. 'Cellitis' perhaps, or anything with the words 'lonely' or 'cold' included in it. The days and weeks passed by and still the door remained closed. I had lost all track of time now, but it was definitely winter, and I had missed my birthday.

My cell door opened suddenly in the middle of the afternoon. It frightened the life out of me, I hadn't heard the guard coming along the corridor. The guard gestured for me to come out and then marched me along several passageways through different cell blocks and down a few flights of stairs.

It was not the way we usually went when they took me for questioning, and I wondered what was going on. I had not been out of the cell for so long now that having to walk this distance was tiring.

A strange noise was getting louder the further we went.

At first, I thought it was a lot of people shouting then I realised there was music also.

What on earth was happening?

It was getting deafening now and I couldn't decide if it was really that loud or just the fact that I had been without sound for so long.

As the guard pushed open the doors in front of me, my ears were assaulted by the deafening thump of loud disco music and I saw in front of me a room full of women shouting, some singing, and some dancing, all of them making noise of one sort or another.

I was in the middle of a strange party. The songs had something familiar about them and I struggled to remember what they reminded me of. It wasn't pop music but something that I couldn't quite put my finger on. What the hell was going on?

I put my hands up to cover my ears and felt the guard's hand on my shoulder, pushing me down onto a chair beside a table. The guard then sat down on the chair next to mine.

With my hands still covering my ears I looked around.

The table in front of me had a selection of little red cakes and jelly plus other party food.

My eyes scanned the rest of the room. Party balloons, streamers, banners, maybe it was somebody's birthday but why was I here? Then I saw it in the corner of the room, and it all became clear.

A decorated Christmas tree.

I could have wept. Now my rest from questioning was obvious; even the police took a holiday at Christmas.

The party was a huge ordeal for me. I couldn't stand the noise, then the realisation that this was my Christmas away from everything I knew and loved really hit me.

I struggled to hold back my tears and wondered how Jim was spending the day. Was he with his family or was he alone like me?How was my own family coping with me being locked up?

Did Jim miss me as much as I was missing him? How long would it be before I saw him again?

Party finally over, I was escorted back to my cold, quiet solitude.

I wondered how long the holiday lasted.

Some nights later while I was trying to sleep upright on the bed, huddled in my only blanket, knees pulled up to my chest, a sudden sharp pain seared across my stomach then another, they started slowly at first but then began getting worse and more frequent. I went across to the toilet, not sure if I was going to be sick or have diarrhoea. I thought diarrhoea was the most likely, so I sat down. The pain was increasing, and I thought I wanted to pee. In the dim moonlight coming through the cell window, I finally realised that I was bleeding.

I pressed the call bell and waited.

I had never pressed the bell before and hoped that whoever was at the other end would realise that it was serious. Nothing happened so, with the pain still getting worse, I pressed the bell again.

The overhead light was turned on from the outside and as the hatch on the cell door was opened, I saw blood on my clothing and tried to explain to the wardress what was happening. She looked through the hatch, saw the blood, then the light was turned off and the hatch was closed, she went away.

She returned a few minutes later, no light this time, just the hatch opening, and a packet of sanitary towels pushed through and then gone again. The pains kept increasing along with the bleeding and as the night wore on, I realized that this wasn't just a period. I tried to remember when I had had my last period, certainly not while I had been in here but when before then? How could I have missed the now obvious fact that I was pregnant?

Along with the increasing pain came the realization that I was losing this baby. I pressed the bell, nothing, I kept my hand on the bell, still nothing. The urge to push was overwhelming and I tried hard to hold it in. The pain was unbearable for the longest time then, when it slowly subsided, I knew that I had lost our first baby.

At some point after this I passed out and spent the remainder of the night on the cell floor.

A ringing in my ears was driving me crazy. I was trying to

sleep but a persistent alarm clock was trying to get me to wake up.

"Go away," I said again and again. Now my eyelids were being forced open, a bright light was being shone into them. I didn't want to wake up.

Slowly coming around, I realised that I was no longer in my cell but in what looked to be a hospital ward.

I had proper sheets and blankets and had on a nightdress. I was warm for the first time in what seemed like forever.

Later that day a doctor appeared who spoke excellent English and I had my first conversation in over two months.

I was still in the prison, just on the hospital wing.

Yes, the baby was gone, and even though I had spent some hours on that freezing floor and lost a good deal of blood, I would be OK with no permanent damage. *Physically maybe*, I thought, *not mentally*.

I would spend weeks, months, and even years re-living that night and the preceding days and blaming myself for what had happened.

If I had eaten more, would it have been different? Why didn't I know I was pregnant? Finally, and worst of all, would I have taken the risk of coming to Hamburg if I had known beforehand that I was expecting?

Then the doctor asked, "Why didn't you ring the bell?" I explained what had occurred and he promised to help as much as he was allowed.

A few days later I was returned to my cell. First job: clean up the cell. The cell was exactly as I had left it.

Second job: try to clean my clothes. I had been given a gown whilst I was on the hospital wing, now I was back to blood-stained clothes.

At least they had brought in an extra blanket, so I wore that for a few days whilst my clothes dried. Still stained with blood, I had no choice but to put them back on and was left with a constant reminder of the painful ordeal I been through.

About a week later the doctor, as promised, had got some help for me and the British consulate came to visit me in my cell.

His expression told me all I needed to know about how I looked, and I was thankful that the cell did not contain a mirror.

Things began to move at last. A lawyer was allowed a weekly visit and brought news of my family. By the middle of February, I was allowed a change of clothes from the items that had been sent to the prison for me; some letters also, no books though.

A trial date was set for the second week of March and my lawyer assured me that everything was ready. I just had to sit and wait now.

I read my letters over and over again until I knew them off by heart. Only ones from friends and family had been allowed, nothing from Jim. A week before the trial date, during his usual visit, my lawyer and I went through everything one last time.

He said, "Your trial will be at 10 o'clock next Monday and they will bring you to the court just after breakfast. I will see you then for a few minutes before it all begins."

Monday morning came and I couldn't bring myself to eat anything at breakfast. My nerves were terrible, and I was yet to fully recover from the miscarriage. I sat looking at the breakfast food and waited for the cell door to open.

Nothing.

The minutes ticked by and slowly rolled into hours.

Still nothing.

Lunch arrived and I tried to speak to the guard, but she ignored me.

I didn't bother going to the door when the hatch opened for the evening meal. I remained still, sitting on the bed. I waited for the hatch to close, then I lay down and cried.

In all the weeks and months that I had spent in this place, I had not shed a single tear. I would not allow myself to cry, let alone allow someone else to be witness to the act. To cry would have been to give in, accept it all and lose hope of ever getting out.

Now I cried for every lost minute in this place and for my lost child, who would never leave here and whose memory would forever be associated with this grim place. The grief was overwhelming. I thought I would lose my mind. At the worst point I seriously considered ending it all.

Morning came as it always does, and the crying had to cease, I didn't want the guards to see just how low I was. Breakfast arrived as normal, as did lunch then dinner.

There was nothing I could do except sit and wait.

Tuesday passed, then Wednesday.

My only hope now was my weekly visit on Thursday from my lawyer. I tried not to depend on that thought too much. I didn't want to raise my hopes and then face another disappointment.

However, at more or less the usual time on Thursday the cell door was opened, and I was escorted to my regular visiting room.

My lawyer was there, as usual, smiling with his hand held out, ready to shake mine. I could have slapped his face. I did not as usual put out my hand to shake his, nor did I smile. He looked puzzled. Clearly my response was not what he was expecting.

Through gritted teeth I said to him, "Why didn't you come on Monday? What happened to my trial?"

He was totally taken aback and said, "But surely you know? I sent you a message. Your trial has been postponed until May."

"No, I did not know. I waited all day Monday and I have been waiting since to find out what is going on," I said, calmer now but still with no idea why it had been postponed;

and if it could happen once, how many more times could it happen?

He explained that the Dutch police had been contacted after our arrest as Elmo was a Dutch national and Jim and I had, at times, lived in a flat in Holland and that they wanted to question us both about other matters that had been committed on Dutch soil before the trial, whatever that may mean.

The good news, though, was that the trial date was now fixed for May, and they would not be able to delay it a second time.

In the meantime, we would both be questioned again.

With the delay and then this new trial date, I would be allowed some extra privileges whilst I was to remain in the prison. For a few hours each morning I would be allowed out of my cell for a shower and to take some exercise outside. Also, for two hours each afternoon I would go to a workroom and be allowed to mix with other female prisoners and do something useful.

True to his word, the following morning I was taken for a shower; the first proper chance I had to wash in over five months. They even supplied shampoo, a towel, and hot water. I would have stayed there all day if they had let me.

Next a walk in the exercise yard. I had been inactive so long that the walk down to the exercise yard was exhausting in itself and with no coat and only lightweight clothes on I froze. It was still cold outside even though winter was nearly over, I regretted not bringing my blanket with me.

The walk itself was farcical. I was handcuffed on either side to a female guard while two male guards walked with us, one in front and one behind. The five of us shuffled in formation on the small circular concrete path whilst overhead a guard with a shotgun watched us steadily from the fortified tower that I could just glimpse from my cell window. We walked like this for about half an hour, managing not to trip each other up along the way. It wasn't what I had expected when I was told that I would be allowed outside. Still, it was good to breathe fresh air again and to be able to look up at the sky.

Lunch – I had an appetite today; I did not dwell on what the lunch might have been, just ate. The trip to see the workroom was the highlight of the day for me, even better than seeing the sky. It was filled with sewing machines. The female guard approached me as I entered the room and took me to a machine and was obviously going to try and teach me how to sew.

Don't bother, it was second nature to me.

Once she saw that I really did know what to do she left me to it. The task at hand: a pile of prison uniforms that all needed repairs of one sort or another. Child's play. About an hour later the pile in front of me was done and folded neatly on the table to the side of the machine.

While doing the repairs I took the opportunity to look around me at all the other machinists. They seemed to be going at a considerably slower pace, maybe I should have slowed down. Too late now, though, it was obvious I had finished. In unison the room of inmates were all looking at the wall to the far end of the room as though there had been some unseen signal that I had missed.

Then I spotted it: a clock on the end wall; it was three o'clock. The machines were all turned off now and there followed an hour of chatting over cups of tea and coffee. A few of them glanced in my direction but mostly ignored me, so I took the opportunity to study them. A motley crew: all in all, a range of ages up to what looked about ninety, but it seemed to me they all looked older than I was. Maybe prison did that to you.

Coffee over, we were all ushered out of the workroom and back to our cells. Everyone was locked up before me. The guard walked me up the last flight of stairs and along the landing to my cell. It was then that I realised that my cell was the only one on this corridor that had a name written on the board outside the cell door. I had a floor to myself.

I was exhausted. It was the most I had done in any one day in a very long time.

For the first time I slept well in this place. *Was that good or bad*, I wondered when I woke up the next morning and realised that a whole night had gone by in one go.

The next few days passed in much the same way and then it was lawyer day again. This time I was pleased to see him and thanked him for my change in circumstances.

He in turn was pleased to see how much better I looked and probably how much better I now smelled as well. Usual stuff over, I spoke to him about the puzzling things in the last few days. He explained, "You are a category A prisoner because of your association with Jim but under German law you are a child and should not be in an adult prison. Also, because there had been an escape from a Belfast prison yard where they used a helicopter to get prisoners out, they were worried it might happen here and they thought Jim was involved." Jim had also escaped from prison himself in the past. This explained a lot.

The following day I was allowed a trip to the prison shop; if you worked you could shop. My luxury buys were so simple: a toothbrush, toothpaste, shampoo, soap, and a very small bar of chocolate. Workshop Saturday, no work Sunday – that was a very long day. How on earth had I survived all those previous long days without losing my sanity? I thought back to other Sundays in Bray and then Kilcoole but had to put the thoughts both good and bad out of my mind. For now, I had to just focus on getting out of here.

Monday morning saw my little procession, not heading to the exercise yard, but back, I thought, to the police station area. I was right.

We ended up in the usual office, usual two German police: one (his name I had found out at some point was Gunther) and policeman number two (whose name I never knew). They were joined by a third man who introduced himself as a Dutch police officer, who for a second looked vaguely familiar. Unlike the other two this man was blond but also with attractive blue eyes. Strange what random thoughts pop into your head, even in these stressful situations. Now all I had to do was remember where had I seen him before?

Then I remembered he had been in The Pink Elephant a few times. On one occasion he had tried to chat me up. He spoke very good English and also German, I learned as he spoke to policeman one and two for a few minutes.

Introductions over, the questioning started. The Dutch officer said he had only a few questions for me but first he wished to tell me some things. Firstly, apart from the drugs that had been found in the car, Elmo had also admitted to being involved in a bombing in Germany.

"What?" Stunned silence from me while he let that piece of news sink in. He quietly carried on telling me that Elmo had done a deal and named 'other people' to lessen his sentence. I had no way of knowing whether any of this was true or not, so I said nothing. He described the day this bombing had happened. I knew it only too well. I had been in the car going to a Dr Hook concert, although Elmo had not been with us. The Dutch officer told me he had been in the helicopter that had been following the car. I still said nothing; this was one for my lawyer to deal with.

Clearly the three men in front of me must have thought that I had known all about it.

How wrong they were.

He asked if I wished to make any comment. "No," I

replied. The pressure was building.

The second piece of news – he looked almost apologetic as he said his next words, as though he hoped his first piece of news would have done the trick and got me talking – was that Zoë was pregnant and Jim was the father. I glanced at Gunther to see if he had known what this Dutch officer was going to tell me and, as I looked at him, straight into those beautiful pale blue eyes, I knew that the Dutch officer was telling me the truth.

How desperate must they have been to get Jim if they would stoop so low as to tell me this now. They must have been told about the miscarriage. I pitied him for doing this to me. My eyes never left his face and slowly he began to disappear. Bit by bit he was getting paler, less distinct, now a pile of sand on the chair and finally one small piece of grit that would blow away and be lost in the dust at the corners of the room and would eventually blow away altogether the next time someone opened the door. A silence had descended over the room. Gunther and number two had clearly known what he was going to tell me, although they could not understand what he actually said. They had watched my reaction to the news with clinical coolness. I now turned my gaze onto Gunther. He too slowly disappeared into a spec of grit, as did number two policeman, and I waited for the door to open and blow them all away. To me they no longer existed.

If the Dutch officer ever asked me the questions he wanted answers to, I have no idea.

I saw nothing nor heard anything that those three men said or did the rest of that day.

Eventually taken back to my cell, I went over what had happened.

After all these months of not talking or giving up the others, they really must have thought they had the final straw that would break my back by telling me about Zoë.

How wrong they had been.

I loved Jim and, although I totally disagreed with how he was going about things, at the same time I also totally agreed with the reasons he was doing it. When you are backed up against a wall you have two choices: you give in, or you fight. He had chosen to fight. I did not blame him or condemn him for that.

The Zoë news was a blow but not unexpected. She had taken her opportunity while she had the chance. I could not worry too much about it at the moment. There was nothing I could do about it anyway.

For now, I needed to concentrate on my upcoming trial and the added dimension that Elmo had now brought to everything.

The next few weeks passed with a steady monotony. At least I could go out of the cell now and I was clean and reasonably warm. My health, physical and mental, had improved and I was once again ready for the upcoming trial.

The big day eventually dawned, and I was led through the

prison cell blocks to the attached court room. There would be five judges, no jury, and I would be tried as a child.

The trial was only expected to last a few days with the verdict and any sentence on the last day; no waiting to find out my fate, just swift, efficient German justice.

As I entered the court room, Elmo was already sitting at the lawyers' table in front of the judges' raised platform. They sat me down at the table next to his and my lawyer joined me. Elmo completely ignored me.

The five judges entered, and we were under way. An interpreter translated the proceedings for me, although he could not keep up with the conversational pace and a lot of the time I was unsure of what was happening.

My lawyer assured me at the end of the day that things had gone well, and the trial would be finished the following day. The judges would ask me a few questions in the morning, and I would have my verdict in the afternoon. He had entered a plea of not guilty on my behalf, although he thought I should have pleaded guilty for a lesser sentence.

Once again, and I hoped for the last time, I told him, "I will not plead guilty to something I have not done."

Exasperated, he shrugged his shoulders and said, "The prosecution has asked for a sentence of 35 years but as you are being tried as a child the maximum would be 20."

Nice to go to bed on a positive note, I could be middle aged before I got out of prison.

The judges' questions the following day were as expected, and I answered them truthfully. I was then taken to a holding cell to have lunch and wait for the verdict, which would definitely be that afternoon.

I looked at my lunch but couldn't eat it, and so began the long wait to see what my future would be.

There were two possible outcomes as I saw it.

Option one: I would receive a long prison sentence which I would have to serve here in Germany with maybe the possibility of returning to England at some point to finish it in an English prison. At least if they sent me back to England at some later date friends and family would be able to come and visit.

Whilst serving my sentence I would receive beautiful love letters from Jim and for the time I was incarcerated I could persuade and console myself with the notion that the only reason we were apart was because I was locked up.

Option two: I would be found not guilty, freed immediately, and would then have to live for the rest of my life without Jim knowing that he and I could not be together, not because he didn't love me but because Zoë and her child would always be between us. I knew in my heart of hearts that Jim would never abandon this longed-for child.

While the judges deliberated over their verdict, I deliberated over the rest of my life. If the choice was up to me which option, would I choose?

I cast my mind back to that spring day so long ago in Bray and all that had happened in between and pondered my options.

Not for the first time I realized, I would have to be really careful what I wished for.

ABOUT THE AUTHOR

T.A. Bannon lives in a small city in southern England.

She has four children and, so far, seven grandchildren.

She is retired and spends her time reading, gardening, doing D.I.Y, babysitting and now writing. This is her first book. She is now busy working on the second one.

Printed in Great Britain
by Amazon